The garage door was closed,
so Joe gave it a loud knock.
"Hey, David!" he called out.
"It's me—Joe! Are you in there?"

There was no answer.

Joe, Sam, and Wishbone walked to the front door of David's house.

Sam rang the doorbell several times. There was no answer there, either.

Joe stuck his hands in his jacket pockets. "Sam, I'm just a little bit worried."

"Yes, so am I," Sam said, putting a hand on Joe's shoulder.

They stood there a moment, not sure what to do next. Even Wishbone seemed a bit confused.

"I mean, it's probably nothing," Sam said hopefully. "It's probably just a silly misunderstanding."

"You know," Joe said, feeling a chill run down his spine, "this is reminding me of *The Mystery of Edwin Drood*. Except, this time, it's not a character in a book who's disappeared—it's our best friend, David."

Other books in the
WISHBONE™ Mysteries series:

*coming soon

WISHBONE Mysteries

CASE OF THE UNSOLVED CASE

by Alexander Steele

WISHBONE™ created by Rick Duffield

Big Red Chair Books™, *A Division of* **Lyrick Publishing**™

This book is a work of fiction. The characters, incidents, and dialogues are products of the author's imagination and are not to be construed as real. Any resemblance to actual events or persons, living or dead, is entirely coincidental.

 Big Red Chair Books™, *A Division of Lyrick Publishing*™
300 E. Bethany Drive, Allen, Texas 75002

©1998 Big Feats! Entertainment

Edited by Kevin Ryan

Copy edited by Jonathon Brodman

Cover concept and design by Lyle Miller

Interior illustrations by Don Adair

Wishbone photograph by Carol Kaelson

Library of Congress Catalog Card Number: 98-84946

ISBN: 1-57064-287-7

First printing: November 1998

10 9 8 7 6 5 4 3 2 1

Printed in the United States of America

To my trusted dog consultants—
Walter, Shijo, Isis, and Jasmine

FROM THE BIG RED CHAIR . . .

Oh . . . hi! Wishbone here. You caught me right in the middle of some of my favorite things—books. Let me welcome you to the WISHBONE MYSTERIES. In each story, I help my human friends solve a puzzling mystery. In *CASE OF THE UNSOLVED CASE*, David suddenly disappears. Joe and I search for our pal, but as the hours tick by, there is no trace of David. . . .

The story takes place early in the winter, during the same time period as the events that you'll see in the second season of my WISHBONE television show. In this story, Joe is fourteen, and he and his friends are in the eighth grade. Like me, they are always ready for adventure . . . and a good mystery.

You're in for a real treat, so pull up a chair and a snack and sink your teeth into *CASE OF THE UNSOLVED CASE!*

Chapter One

A winter wind howled through the trees. Outside the window, Wishbone could see the leafless limbs sway back and forth against a background of dark sky.

It's a great night to be inside, the white-with-brown-and-black-spots Jack Russell terrier thought. *Unless you happen to be a Siberian husky.*

Wishbone was lying comfortably at one end of the living room couch. At the other end lay Wishbone's best buddy, Joe Talbot. Joe was a good-natured fourteen-year-old boy with a truly noble heart. He had straight brown hair, broad shoulders, and a great smile. He was also a top athlete, almost as good at basketball as Wishbone was at stick-chasing.

Wishbone looked around the living room, admiring the cozy furniture and handsome wood paneling. The dog wasn't talking much, because Joe was concentrating on reading a book.

Wishbone knew the book was *The Mystery of Edwin Drood,* by Charles Dickens. It was one of the dog's favorites. Wishbone felt a slight shiver run through his fur. He knew this was one of the most mysterious books ever written. Joe was reading the book as part of a school assignment the students had been given to complete during the school's winter break.

Wishbone glanced toward another window. He watched a limb sway in the wind. Its gray branches reminded him of a witch's crooked fingers. The wind whistled and whooshed in a way Wishbone was certain he had never heard before.

This is also a great night for reading a mystery, Wishbone thought. *With all that blowing, I almost get the feeling there's a real-life mystery in the air—something dark and dangerous, filled with doom. Whoa! I'd better stop this. I'm beginning to scare myself.*

Wishbone turned to look at a happier sight, the family Christmas tree. Like most dogs, Wishbone had a great liking for trees. But Christmas trees, with their glittering tinsel and twinkling lights, were extra-special.

That's right, Wishbone remembered. *It's only ten days until Christmas.*

Wishbone raised his always alert ears as he heard the back door open. The dog announced, "Ellen's home!"

A few moments later, Joe's mom, Ellen, came through the study and then entered the living room. A slender woman with thick brown hair, Ellen was a librarian and amateur writer. She knew more about books than anyone Wishbone knew—not counting himself, of course.

Ellen set down several shopping bags on the floor. Then she hung up her coat and said, "Hi, Joe."

Joe looked up briefly from his book. "Hi, Mom."

Hmm . . . Wishbone thought, his eyes glued to the bags. *It's only ten days until Christmas, and Ellen comes home with a bunch of bags. And I can smell that those aren't grocery bags. They're regular shopping bags. It doesn't take a detective like Sherlock Holmes to figure out what's in them. Presents!*

"You must really be enjoying that story," Ellen told

Joe. "You look as if you're concentrating on a free-throw shot. I've never seen you so wrapped up in a book before."

"Uh-huh," Joe murmured, as he turned another page.

Ellen smiled. Then she picked up the shopping bags and walked down the hall.

Wishbone jumped off the couch and trotted after Ellen. "Oh, Ellen, let me give you a paw with those bags. I've got four good ones, you know."

Ellen stopped when she came to the doorway of the study. "Sorry, Wishbone, I've got some secret business to take care of in here."

Wishbone raised himself up on his hind legs. "But I love secrets. No one keeps a secret better than—"

Ellen shut the door to the study.

Wishbone went back down on all fours. *Yes, I know what that secret business is. Ellen is hiding the presents in there.* If Wishbone was lucky, Ellen wouldn't wrap them just yet. That way, he would still have a chance to catch an early peek at them.

Suddenly, the dog heard footsteps coming toward the front porch. In the best canine manner, Wishbone had a highly developed sense of hearing. He ran toward the front door. Soon he picked up the scents of two very familiar humans. He also had a great sense of smell.

"It's David and Sam," Wishbone called to Joe.

The doorbell rang.

"Who is it?" Joe shouted at the door.

"I just *told* you who it is," Wishbone said. "It's David and Sam!"

"It's me—David," a voice answered from outside. "Sam is here, too."

"See? I told you," Wishbone said with a frustrated sigh. "Why is it that no one ever listens to the dog?"

"Come on in," Joe called out.

The front door opened. Wishbone saw two of his best pals, Sam Kepler and David Barnes. They were both

Joe's age, and they went to Sequoyah Middle School with Joe. Both kids gave Wishbone a greeting scratch behind his ears. Then they went into the living room and took off their jackets.

"*Brrr!* It's really cold outside," Sam said. She rubbed her hands together to warm them.

Sam Kepler, whose real name was Samantha, was an outgoing girl with a warm personality. She had silky blond hair and very pretty hazel eyes. Sam also had lots of artistic talent. Perhaps Sam's best quality was that she was always willing to help a person or dog in need.

"I see you're reading *The Mystery of Edwin Drood*," David told Joe. "Sam and I both finished it earlier today."

David lived next door to Joe. He had curly black hair and dark eyes that showed a lot of curiosity. He was an absolute whiz with anything electrical, mechanical, or generally scientific. Wishbone always found a visit to David's garage laboratory an exciting experience.

"David and I figured we'd stop by before heading over to Miss Gilmore's house," Sam said.

Joe kept his eyes on his book. "Make yourself at home. I'm just a few pages from the end of the story, and I want to finish it."

Sam took David's arm and led him into the dining room. Not wanting to miss any action, Wishbone followed. "I need to ask you something," Sam told David in a low voice. "This year I'm making all my Christmas presents. But I don't know what I should make for Joe. I thought you might have some ideas."

"I don't know what to give him, either," David said, also in a low voice. "I want to get him an extra-nice present this year."

"Why is that?" Sam asked.

David and Sam took seats at the dining room table. Wishbone sat nearby on the floor. "A few days ago," David said, "Joe and I went biking around town. We were

11

just goofing off. And Joe lost something that was very important to him."

"What?" Sam asked.

"A gold high-school class ring that belonged to his father," David replied.

Sam showed a look of great concern. "Oh, that's a shame."

"It certainly is," Wishbone added. This was the first he had heard about the missing ring. The dog knew how much Joe cared for anything that had belonged to his father. Steve Talbot had died from a rare blood disease when Joe was only six years old.

"How did he lose it?" Sam asked.

"It was the first day Joe ever wore the ring," David explained. "His finger had finally gotten big enough for it. But maybe his finger still wasn't *quite* the right size, because the ring fell off somewhere. The problem is, we couldn't find it anywhere."

"Maybe I could help you search for the ring," Sam suggested.

David shook his head. "It's no use. Joe and I retraced our steps and did a really careful search. Then, I felt so badly, the next day I spent several hours retracing our steps again. I couldn't find that ring anywhere. Maybe someone found it and took it, or maybe it rolled under something. Anyway, that's why I want to get Joe a really nice present."

"Okay," Sam said, "I'll try to think of something really cool for you to give Joe."

"And I'll do the same for you," David said.

"Maybe one of you could get Joe a nice rubber chew toy," Wishbone suggested. "You know, the kind that squeaks when you bite on it. But then . . . I don't know if he likes those as much as I do."

Sam stood up. "Come on, let's go back to the living room before Joe realizes we're talking about him."

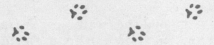

As David, Sam, and Wishbone went back to the living room, Joe closed his book with a thump. "Done," he declared. "I have officially finished reading *The Mystery of Edwin Drood.*"

David and Sam sat down. Wishbone rested his furred belly on the rug. "You mean, at least as much as it's possible to finish it," Sam commented.

Joe knew exactly what Sam was referring to. Charles Dickens had died before he finished writing the novel. This would have been bad enough with a regular book. But in the case of *Edwin Drood,* it was really frustrating because the book was a mystery. In fact, the class's assignment was to read the book and then figure out how they thought the author meant for the story to end.

"I thought it was a great book," Joe said. He ran his eyes over the gold-colored letters of the title on the cover. "I couldn't stop turning the pages. But this school assignment isn't going to be so easy. There are a lot of possible solutions to this story."

"The teacher said we could discuss ideas," David pointed out. "Maybe the three of us should get together one day and do that."

"That's a great idea," Sam said with enthusiasm. "When is a good time for you two?"

"How about tomorrow?" David said. "Not too early, though. One of the best things about school breaks is that you get to sleep late."

"How about tomorrow at noon?" Joe suggested. "My house."

"Great!" Sam and David said together. Even Wishbone wagged his tail excitedly at the idea.

The doorbell rang.

13

"I wonder who that is," Joe said as he got up off the couch.

When he opened the front door, he saw one of his schoolmates on the porch, Chloe Devine. This was surprising, because Joe never spent any time with Chloe.

"Hi, there," Chloe greeted Joe in a cheerful voice. "I was looking for David. I went to his house, and his mother said he would be over here. So here I am."

Chloe had frizzy blond hair, and eyes so blue they might have been marbles. She seemed to be in a great mood ninety-nine percent of the time. Another thing about Chloe was that she had the reputation of being a bit of a flirt.

"Uh . . . well . . . come on in," Joe said with some hesitation.

"Oh, thanks," Chloe said brightly. She followed Joe into the living room. Sam and David both greeted Chloe. Joe could see that they were also surprised by her sudden appearance.

Chloe sat on the couch next to David. She turned her blue eyes toward him and said, "I was looking for you."

"Why were you looking for me?" David asked.

Chloe gave a little laugh, which sounded a bit like a bird chirping. "No special reason. I just wanted to see how you are. So . . . how are you?"

"I'm just fine," David said, seeming a little bit uncomfortable.

Sam gave Joe a meaningful look, which he figured meant something like: "I think Chloe has a crush on our friend."

Ellen, who had gone upstairs, called down, "Okay, everyone, it's time to get going. We're supposed to be there at seven."

The kids stood up, and Chloe asked, "Where are all of you going?"

14

"We're going next door to Wanda Gilmore's house," David replied. "She's having a few people over."

"Oh," Chloe said, sounding disappointed.

After an awkward silence, David said, "I . . . uh . . . guess it's okay if you want to come along, too."

Chloe's face lit up like a lightbulb. "I'd just love to!"

Ellen came into the living room, and Joe introduced her to Chloe. Then everyone put on their jackets and began to head out the front door. Wishbone joined the others, but Joe noticed that David wasn't with the group. For some reason, he was hanging back by the fireplace, looking out the window with a strange expression on his face.

"Uh . . . David," Joe said quietly, "is anything wrong?"

David turned around, as if startled. "Uh . . . no. Of course not."

"You're not still feeling badly about what happened to the ring, are you? I told you not to worry about it."

"No, I wasn't thinking about the ring."

"Is it Chloe?" Joe asked.

"No," David insisted. "I'm telling you, nothing is wrong."

Joe was not convinced. David had been his neighbor for quite a while. In that time, he had seen David nearly every day, and in practically every kind of situation. If anyone knew whether there was something bothering David, it was Joe.

"Well, look," Joe said, "if you want—"

"Come on," David said, moving away from the fireplace. "Let's go over to Miss Gilmore's."

Joe watched David put on his jacket and walk out of the house. A cold burst of wind blew through the open doorway, ruffling Joe's hair.

It's always hard when one of your friends is going

15

through a difficult time, Joe thought, as he smoothed his hair back in place. *But it's even harder when he or she won't let you in on what it is. Oh, well . . . I'll get to the bottom of whatever this is, sooner or later.*

Joe followed David out the door.

Chapter Two

"Hello, everybody!" Wanda Gilmore cried out as she opened her door. "Come on in! It's so windy out there."

"Don't mind if we do," Wishbone said. He led Ellen, Joe, Sam, David, and Chloe into Wanda's living room.

As Wanda took everyone's jackets, Joe introduced her to Chloe. Wishbone liked Wanda, who was a lively woman with unusual taste in clothing. At the moment, she was wearing a brightly colored sweater, along with tight, striped pants. She had all sorts of interests, and belonged to many organizations. In fact, Wishbone knew the real reason for this get-together was to discuss Oakdale's annual Christmas-tree-lighting ceremony. Wanda was always in charge of this event.

As the humans greeted one another, Wishbone checked out the room with his sharp eyes. There was a lot of interesting stuff in Wanda's house—Persian carpets, lacy curtains, modern artwork. The dog's eyes fell on something of even greater interest than the furnishings of Wanda's house. Sitting on a low table were onion dip, carrot slices, and a bowl overflowing with salty-scented potato chips.

Sitting right by the food was Mr. Pruitt. He was a

pleasant man with a plump shape that was a bit like a comfortably stuffed pillow. Mr. Pruitt had taught sixth-grade English to Joe. Wishbone knew that Mr. Pruitt and Wanda had actually gone on a few dates together.

Mr. Pruitt stood, holding a carrot slice with dip on the tip. "I hope you don't mind, but I started on the snacks without you."

"Of course I mind," Wishbone said, as he made a beeline for the food. "But I'll forgive you, as long as you promise to be generous."

Mr. Pruitt noticed the dog staring at the chips. "Uh . . . is it all right if I give the dog a chip?"

"Just one," Ellen said with amusement. "We don't want to make a beggar out of him."

"Hey, I was *born* to be a beggar," Wishbone said, rising to his hind legs. "Begging is what I do best!"

Mr. Pruitt picked out a large potato chip and offered it to Wishbone.

In less than five seconds, the chip was crunched, chewed, and swallowed. "Thanks," Wishbone said, his tail wagging happily. "How about another?"

Mr. Pruitt didn't respond. Everyone sat down. Wishbone parked himself on the floor right next to Mr. Pruitt. He figured the man might weaken at some point and send a few more chips his way.

Wanda set a note pad on her lap and acted in a businesslike manner. "Okay, let's talk about the tree-lighting ceremony. It's this Friday, remember? That's just two days away. We should all meet at ten o'clock that day to do the decorating. The tree is already in place, and I've got all the decorations ready. Except, Ellen, I think you said you would make the strings of popcorn."

Wishbone licked his chops. "Ah, yes! Popcorn!"

"Yes, I will," Ellen replied.

"And David," Wanda mentioned, "you said you

would work with the volunteer electricians on the wiring and electrical power."

"Right," David said.

Chloe smiled brightly at David. "When it comes to all that mechanical stuff, David's the best, isn't he?"

David shifted uncomfortably in his seat.

"Oh, no," Wishbone said under his breath. "This girl's got it bad for David. That's not good."

Mr. Pruitt raised a hand. "Wanda, what about my Santa Claus costume?"

"I'm picking it up tomorrow afternoon," Wanda answered. "There is one other important thing I want to discuss. This year, I'd like to do something really exciting at the ceremony. But, the thing is, I don't know what that is yet."

Mr. Pruitt raised his hand again. "I'm going to dress up as Santa and read the poem *A Visit from St. Nicholas.* Isn't that exciting enough?"

"Oh, that's very exciting," Wanda said, keeping her businesslike tone. "I wouldn't miss it for the world, Bob. But you do that *every* year. This time I want to add something else. I want it to be something unique or really modern—maybe even spectacular. Any bright ideas?"

As everyone tried to think of unusual ideas, Wishbone listened to the wind howling outside. *That wind is beginning to make me a little uncomfortable,* Wishbone thought. *It doesn't sound like regular wind. It sounds like . . . weird wind. Who knows what it's blowing into town?*

"I have an idea," Ellen said finally. "I don't know if it's spectacular, but it could be sweet. We could make up a bunch of little treat packages for the smaller kids. You know, candy and little toys. We'll wrap them up and pass them out during the ceremony."

"Well, that's not bad," Wanda said, twirling a pen in her hand. "But it still needs some more excitement. . . . I know! We could have elves pass around the packages. In fact, the elves could be played by Joe, Sam, David, and Chloe!"

Sam made a face. "I don't know, Miss Gilmore. I think we might be a bit too old for that. Besides, it's the kind of thing that would take us a while to live down at school."

"Like several decades," David added.

Chloe let out a high-pitched laugh that caused Wishbone to fold down his ears. "David, I never knew you were so funny!"

"I understand," Wanda said with a sympathetic nod. "Playing elves might not be good for your image. Okay, then, I just need to locate a few elves somewhere else."

Mr. Pruitt gave an upset shrug. "I thought my Santa act was plenty spectacular. But if we have to have elves, we'll have elves."

There was a knock at the door.

Wishbone sprang to his feet. "Hey! Maybe that's the pizza-delivery elves. Did anyone order pizza?"

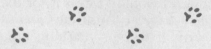

As Wanda got up and opened the front door, Joe felt a gust of wind.

Wanda let in Mrs. Hernandez, a middle-aged woman who lived on the block. Joe thought she was a nice neighbor. But there had been one time when she lost her temper—when she wrongly suspected Wishbone had made a mess of her front porch.

A boy and girl followed Mrs. Hernandez into Wanda's house. Joe guessed that they were about his own age. They looked like each other. Both kids had athletic builds, and glossy black hair.

"I want everyone to meet my niece and nephew, Lola and Luis," Mrs. Hernandez told the group. "Lola is fourteen, and Luis is fifteen. Their parents are shopping around right now for a house in Cincinnati, so the kids are staying here with me for the holidays. Wanda asked me to stop by so Luis and Lola could meet the other kids in the neighborhood."

While Wanda took her new guests' jackets, everyone introduced themselves. "What a neat house," Lola said. She began to move around the living room, examining everything. "These decorations are great! And, oh, this is fabulous artwork!"

Joe could see that Lola was full of energy and friendliness. He liked her right away. Luis, on the other hand, just stood there, silent. He was quite tall, and he wore a black-leather jacket, which he wouldn't take off. Joe sensed the boy had a "too cool" attitude.

"Are you two moving to Cincinnati?" Joe asked.

"Yes," Lola said, as she picked up a small piece of sculpture. "My dad works for a company that is always sending us to live in different places. So every few years we move to a different city. That's us. Always on the move."

"That must be very interesting," Mr. Pruitt said. "Seeing all those different places."

"Where have you lived?" Ellen asked Luis.

Luis seemed bored, as if he had been asked that same question many times. "Arizona, Pennsylvania, Missouri, and Florida."

After a few more questions, the adults moved to one side of the room. The kids and Wishbone moved to the other side. Luis leaned against a wall. Chloe stuck right by David's side, as if they were glued together.

"How did you like Arizona?" Sam asked Luis and Lola.

"It's really hot there," Lola said, kneeling down to pet Wishbone. "But the desert is so beautiful. And we got to camp out at the Grand Canyon a few times. The Grand

Canyon is fantastic. . . . What a cute dog this is. It's a Jack Russell terrier, right?"

"That's right," Joe said. He could see that Wishbone had taken a liking to Lola. "His name is Wishbone."

"I've always wanted to see the Grand Canyon," David said.

"What a coincidence!" Chloe exclaimed. "Me, too!"

Joe tried to include Luis in the conversation. "Luis, when you were in Florida, did you ever go scuba-diving?"

"Yeah, lots of times," Luis said casually. "We lived right near the Gulf Coast. It's got some of the best coral reefs in the world. There are also some old, sunken ships around there. You're supposed to stay clear of them, but of course I didn't. . . . So what do you guys do for excitement in this town? It looks kind of quiet."

"Do you like basketball?" Joe asked.

"Let me explain something," Lola said humorously. "When my brother says 'excitement,' he really means danger. He's what you might call the daredevil type."

"What about the town water tower?" Luis said, folding his arms across his leather jacket. "Have any of you ever climbed to the top of it?"

"I'm afraid not," Sam said. "It's awfully high."

"Oh, just thinking about that makes me dizzy," Chloe said with a shudder.

"The higher, the better," Luis said, bragging. "Maybe I'll climb it while I'm in this area."

"Uh . . . maybe you shouldn't," David suggested. "You might get hurt."

Luis fixed his eyes on David. "I see you're the type who likes to play it safe."

"Luis," Lola scolded, "that's not nice."

"I don't always play things safe," David told Luis. "I just don't play things that are, well . . . stupid."

Instantly, a glare formed in Luis's eyes. "Are you calling me stupid?"

Joe watched the scene carefully. He knew David hadn't meant to offend Luis. David was always polite.

"No, I wasn't calling you stupid," David insisted. "I was only saying you shouldn't climb the water tower."

Luis pushed away from the wall and took a few threatening steps toward David. "Look," he said in a low voice, "I don't like to be called stupid."

"No one does," David said calmly. "And if I gave you the wrong impression, I'm sorry."

Luis and David stared at each other for a tense moment. Baring his teeth, Wishbone gave Luis a low growl.

Things were getting off to a bad start with Luis, Joe thought. He could tell that Luis and Lola were interesting kids, and he wanted to make them both feel welcome in Oakdale.

"Hey," Joe said, stepping between the two boys, "maybe we should all get together while you are in town. There's no Grand Canyon around here, but I'm sure we could find something that's fun to do."

"How about tomorrow?" Lola said eagerly.

"Uh . . . any day but tomorow," Sam said, waving a hand in the air. "You see, we've got this assignment for school. We set aside tomorrow to work on it. I'm not sure how long it will take. Just to be safe . . . I mean, just to be sure, why don't we make plans for another day?"

Luis shrugged and went back to leaning against the wall.

"Okay," Lola said, giving Sam a friendly pat on the back. "We'll give you a call."

"Are you talking about the *Edwin Drood* assignment?" Chloe asked.

"Uh . . . yes," Joe said, realizing that Chloe had not been invited to join in.

"Oh, can I come, too?" Chloe asked. "Don't forget, I have the same assignment."

Joe decided to let David handle the request, in case he didn't want Chloe to bother him during the discussion.

David scratched his neck. Then he said, "Sure, I guess you can come. "Meet us at Joe's house tomorrow at noon."

"Thanks," Chloe said cheerfully.

Just then, Mr. Pruitt came over. Joe saw Wishbone scamper over to search for any crumbs Mr. Pruitt might have left where he had been sitting.

"David," Mr. Pruitt said, taking David's arm, "could I talk to you about something? Maybe we should go in the next room. It's sort of a private matter."

"Oh, don't be long," Chloe said, grabbing at the sleeve of David's other arm.

"Okay, okay," David said, as he slipped out of Chloe's grasp.

Joe watched Mr. Pruitt and David pass through the hanging glass beads that separated Wanda's dining room from the living room. Immediately, the two began a conversation. Mr. Pruitt seemed very concerned about

24

something. David listened with a curious expression. Joe strained to hear, but there was too much noise in the living room for him to catch the words.

Joe watched a tree swaying wildly in the wind outside the window. *Something seems weird about this evening,* he thought. *All the weirdness centers around David. First, he seems to have something on his mind that he won't talk about. Now it seems as if David is a magnet, drawing all these different people to him for different reasons—Chloe, Luis, Mr. Pruitt. What's going on?*

Several hours later, Joe lay snugly under the covers of his bed. The wind blew so hard that the branches of a tree were scraping against the side of the house, creating a very creepy sound. But Joe always felt safe among the familiar things in his bedroom—the pennants, trophies, photographs, and, of course, Wishbone, who lay asleep at Joe's feet.

Joe's mind kept moving through *The Mystery of Edwin Drood* as if he were still reading the book's words. The author had painted the story with such rich detail that everything stayed real and clear in Joe's mind.

Joe picked up the book, which lay on the floor beside his bed. It was an old book with a worn-down cover and faded pages. The book had belonged to Joe's father when he was a boy. When Joe touched his father's belongings, he got a sense that his father was a little bit with him, even though he was no longer alive. Joe still felt badly about losing his dad's school ring, but he hoped it might turn up sooner or later.

Joe flipped through the book and stopped at a page with a black-and-white ink illustration. The picture showed an old jeweler handing a pocket watch to Edwin

Drood. Edwin was a handsome young man dressed in the style of the nineteenth century in England. A caption showed what the jeweler was saying: "Twenty minutes past two, Mr. Drood, I set your watch at. Let me recommend you not to let it run down, sir."

Even though Joe was warm, he suddenly shivered. He knew that a few pages later, Edwin would end up missing, and that the novel would end before his disappearance could be explained. There was something haunting about this fact. Not only did Edwin Drood disappear from the plot, but, also, because Dickens didn't finish the book, Edwin Drood would never be found. His whereabouts would remain a mystery . . . forever.

Chapter Three

The next morning, Wishbone had the house all to himself. He was roaming around the kitchen searching for any crumbs that might have been left on the floor from breakfast, but there was nothing. Unfortunately, Ellen kept the place much too clean for the dog's taste.

Hmm . . . what else should I do? Wishbone wondered. *Ellen's at the library for the day, and Joe's out shopping for some Christmas presents. Hey—presents! Yes! I still haven't gotten a peek at those presents Ellen brought home!*

Wishbone hurried out of the kitchen and trotted down the hall. He pushed open the study door with his muzzle and went inside. *Now, where would Ellen have hidden my present?* Wishbone thought, glancing around the room. *She knows I can get into the closet, so that idea is no good. Let's see. . . . What would be the best possible hiding place in this room? . . . Oooh, I know! Behind the books. Excellent, Ellen. Terrific hiding place. Too bad I'm one step ahead of you.*

One wall of the room was filled from floor to ceiling with bookcases loaded with books. Wishbone went to the lowest bookshelf and managed to pull out a few books with his front paw. He created an opening right next to *The Collected Works of William Shakespeare.*

"Oh, present, present, where art thou?" Wishbone whispered, as he stuck his muzzle inside the opening.

No presents here, Wishbone thought, as he pulled his muzzle out. *I bet Ellen didn't hide my present on the lowest shelf because she figured that would be too easy for me. Ten to one, she went for a higher shelf. She doesn't think I could get that high. But, oh-ho-ho, she doesn't know how clever I can be.*

Wishbone climbed up on a footstool. From there, he leaped up onto Ellen's desk. He walked across some papers, a few pens, the computer keyboard, and the telephone answering machine. He came to his big red chair. After stepping on top of the chair, he pawed out a few books from the bookshelf, right above his chair. The books tumbled to the floor. Wishbone stuck his muzzle into the opening, right beside the great whaling novel, *Moby Dick*.

Wishbone saw a small plastic bag. He grabbed it between his teeth and jumped down onto the chair's seat. He worked an object out of the bag with his paw.

"There she blows!" Wishbone barked out.

It was a big rawhide bone twisted into the shape of a pretzel. Wishbone's nose could tell right away that the bone was filled through and through with a nice strong beefy flavor.

"Way to go, Ellen! This is a fabulous present!"

Now that his mission had been accomplished, Wishbone knew it was time to return the present to its hiding place. But he couldn't quite bring himself to do it. Not just yet. The bone was just too deliciously tempting.

Maybe I could chew on it for just a few minutes. Yes, that's a good idea. But I'd better not do it here. Joe's due back any minute, and he might catch me in the act. I'd better take this bone to a safer place.

Wishbone stuffed the plastic bag behind the chair's cushion. Then he took the bone in his mouth. He jumped off the chair, ran out of the room, and darted down the hallway. He didn't stop until he had passed through his doggie door at the back of the house.

The day wasn't as windy as the night before had been. Still, the winter air was brisk. "Hey, it's chilly out here," Wishbone told himself. "Maybe I'd better put on my fur coat. . . . Oh, right—I'm already wearing it."

Wishbone ran to the backyard of Wanda's house. Throughout Wanda's yard were all sorts of fresh dirt gardens where Wanda kept a variety of flowers in warmer weather. The gardens' real purpose, however, was to be a burial ground for Wishbone's valuable bone and toy collection.

Wishbone dropped the rawhide bone on the ground, right near a fountain that had a yellow statue of an elephant on it. The dog lay down, holding the bone steady with his front paws.

Ah, yes, Wishbone thought as he began to gnaw. *That beef flavor is just the best!*

Within seconds, Wishbone looked up to see Sparkey, a large golden retriever who lived in the neighborhood.

Wishbone liked Sparkey. The two dogs had shared some fun adventures together.

"Hey, there, Sparkey," Wishbone greeted his friend. "How's it going?"

Sparkey lowered his head to examine the bone.

"Now, look," Wishbone said, keeping the bone safely under a paw. "I'm really not at liberty to share this with you. Sorry, but I'm sure you'll understand."

Sparkey licked his chops. He had a very hungry look in his eyes. Wishbone knew Sparkey had an appetite every bit as powerful as his own.

"Sparkey," Wishbone warned, "don't even *think* what I think you're thinking. Okay?"

Sparkey showed a blank look, as if he didn't really understand what Wishbone had said.

"Sparkey, read my lips," Wishbone said. "I can't—"

Suddenly, Wishbone stuck his black nose in the air. He was picking up the unmistakable scent of cat. He looked around. Sure enough, he saw an unfamiliar gray cat slinking by on the far side of the yard. Wishbone had an interesting relationship with members of the feline species. He disliked their superior attitude, but he loved to chase them.

"Pssst!" Wishbone whispered to Sparkey. "I think we have a visitor."

Sparkey looked at the cat curiously.

The cat focused a pair of glowing green eyes on the two dogs.

Wishbone went into a crouching position. Sparkey did the same. "One, two, three . . . go!" Wishbone called. Like horses out of the gate at a racetrack, Wishbone and Sparkey dashed after the cat.

As the two dogs ran, the cat flew into the front yard, zigzagged around a few gardens, then raced back into the backyard. The cat stopped when she came to a wooden fence. Wishbone and Sparkey both stopped a short distance away. Wishbone trotted to the other side of the yard until he and Sparkey were cutting off both of the yard's escape routes.

"All right," Wishbone said, his pink tongue panting. "We've got her up against a wall, eh, Sparkey?"

Sparkey panted eagerly.

Hearing a window open, Wishbone turned to see Wanda stick her head out of her house. "Listen, you two," Wanda said firmly, "I don't mind if you play in my yard, but I don't want you anywhere near my gardens. Is that understood?"

"Yes, sure, we get the message," Wishbone said, turning back to the cat.

"I mean it," Wanda said, before she finally closed the window.

"Let's move in on the target," Wishbone told Sparkey. "You go from the left, and I'll come from the right. Ready, set . . . go!"

Wishbone and Sparkey dashed for the cat, which raced straight ahead. All three creatures soon met in the middle of one of Wanda's gardens. The chase was so quick that Wishbone wasn't sure exactly what had happened.

There was a cat screech, flying dirt, a big flower bulb shooting through the air, and an animal's paw in Wishbone's face.

When the chase was over, Wishbone and Sparkey were still in the garden. The cat was scampering up the trunk of a tree. Wishbone watched as she disappeared high up in the bare branches.

Wishbone brushed some dirt off his muzzle with a paw. "Well, I guess that's it for now, Sparkey. Once the cat goes up the tree, the dogs are out of luck."

Sparkey looked at Wishbone blankly, as if to say, "What?"

Wishbone heard a spinning tire sound. He recognized it as Joe's bicycle. "Okay," Wishbone told his canine companion. "I've gotta go now. Some humans and I have a book discussion scheduled for noon. See ya!"

Wishbone ran toward the Talbot house. He met Joe in the driveway. "Hi, Wishbone," Joe said, climbing off his bike. "I hope you stayed out of trouble this morning."

Suddenly, Wishbone remembered the rawhide bone.

"Uh . . . look," Wishbone told Joe. "I've got to check on something really quick. I'll meet you inside."

As Joe walked his bike toward the garage, Wishbone spun around. He ran for the spot where he had left the bone. But, surprisingly, the bone wasn't there. Wishbone knew he was in the right spot, because he was right next to the elephant fountain. It was the only elephant fountain in the whole yard. Wishbone walked around a bit. He searched the ground with his eyes and nose. Still, no bone appeared.

This is definitely where I left the bone, Wishbone thought with confusion. *But the bone is definitely not here.*

Wishbone scanned the area in all directions. There was not a soul in sight now—not human, beast, or otherwise.

Wishbone gave his side a thoughtful scratch.

Uh-oh . . . I've got a big problem here. I've got to find that bone before Ellen discovers that it's missing. The good news is, Ellen won't be back from the library until around six. That's plenty of time to solve the situation. Right now, I'd better get home. Those kids are going to need my help with their homework assignment.

Chapter Four

"Come on, folks," Wishbone urged from his seat on the oval rug in the middle of the living room. "Let's get this show on the road. I'm ready for some high-powered intellectual action!"

Joe, Sam, and Chloe were also seated in the room, but none of them responded.

"Okay, maybe *you're* not ready yet," Wishbone muttered. He lay down, figuring that the discussion would not get moving until David showed up. Wishbone listened to the steady ticking of the hallway clock. The dog's hearing was so sharp that each tick sounded like the whack of a hammer.

After seven ticks, Chloe said cheerfully, "I wonder where David is."

"So do I," Sam said, glancing at her watch. "He's usually on time. But it's a quarter past twelve, and he's still not here. This whole session was David's idea in the first place."

"Maybe he found some good crumbs to nibble in his kitchen," Wishbone suggested. "If he's lucky, his mom isn't such a great housekeeper."

"Let me give him a call," Joe said, getting to his feet. He left the room, then returned a few moments later.

"Was he home?" Sam asked.

Joe shook his head. "There was no answer at the Barnes house. And I checked our answering machine to see if he might have left a message. But there wasn't a single message."

Wishbone listened as another ten ticks hammered on the clock.

Chloe examined her fingernails, which were painted with pink polish. "I sure hope nothing has happened to David. I was looking forward so much to seeing him today. He's such a neat guy. Everything about him is so neat. Don't you think David is neat?"

"Yes, we think he's neat," Sam said, hiding a smile.

"I think he's really neat, too," Chloe continued. "I hope he thinks I'm neat."

Wishbone glanced up at Chloe. "Kid, I think you're barking up the wrong tree. Somehow, I don't think you're David's type. You're just a bit too . . . too . . . well, *too something.*"

The clock continued to tick. . . .

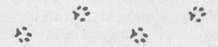

David's lateness was starting to make Joe concerned, but he told himself not to worry. He slapped his leg and said, "So, why don't we start the discussion without David? We can get him caught up as soon as he gets here."

"Good idea," Sam agreed. "How should we go about this?"

Joe was looking forward to this discussion. Because Charles Dickens had died before completing *The Mystery of Edwin Drood,* no one would ever know the book's ending. But Joe was very interested in figuring out what that outcome *might* be.

"Our assignment," Joe said, taking charge, "is to

figure out how we think Charles Dickens wanted *The Mystery of Edwin Drood* to end. The most important issues we have to deal with are these: What happened to Edwin Drood? And who is the man in disguise who goes by the name of Dick Datchery?"

"I have a suggestion," Sam said, twirling a strand of her blond hair. "The plot of this book is very complicated. Maybe we should review the story's basic ideas first."

"Sounds fine with me," Chloe said, checking her pink fingernails.

"Joe, why don't you start?" Sam said.

Wishbone cocked an ear to the conversation.

Joe cleared his throat. "All right. Well, the story takes place in England in the 1800s. Most of the story happens in a small village called Cloisterham. And . . . uh . . . the first character we meet is John Jasper."

"Tell us about him," Sam said, leaning forward with interest.

"John Jasper is the choir leader at the cathedral," Joe explained. "He's a respected man in town, but . . . he has a dark secret. You see, he's fed up with his dull life in his dull town. So, on certain nights, he leaves Cloisterham."

"Where does he go?" Chloe asked, looking up from her fingernails.

Joe was pleased to see that he had caught the attention of Sam and Chloe. He turned up the collar of his shirt and lowered his voice. "On certain nights, John Jasper makes his way to London. He creeps to the worst area of the city and enters an opium den. There he smokes a pipe filled with opium, which is a type of drug that puts him in a weird trance."

Getting involved with the story, Sam and Chloe both made a low, moaning sound. Joe knew they were imitating the sounds Jasper made when he was in an opium trance.

Joe returned his shirt collar to its normal position.

36

"But, by morning, Jasper always returns to Cloisterham, acting completely innocent. He acts as if he never left his bed. But, you see, the opium takes its toll on him. You get the impression that it's making him go a little crazy."

"Ooh! I like characters who go crazy," Chloe said, clapping her hands. "Now, what about Edwin Drood? He's a neat character."

Joe held up a finger. "Edwin Drood is Jasper's nephew. A few days before Christmas, Edwin comes to visit Cloisterham."

Wishbone rose eagerly to his feet and trotted over to Joe. He offered a paw, which Joe shook.

Chloe let out one of her chirping laughs. "It looks like the dog wants to play the part of Edwin."

"That's just like Wishbone," Sam said. "He always wants to be the star."

Joe spoke to Wishbone, pretending they were characters in the book. "Hello, there, my dear nephew, Edwin. It is jolly good to see you, old boy."

Wishbone looked up at Joe, almost as if he were saying something in reply.

Chloe left her seat and knelt down to wrap her arms around Wishbone's neck and hug him. "Now, let's not forget the romantic part of the book. Edwin Drood has a fiancée."

Wishbone looked as if he was worried.

"Tell us about her," Sam told Chloe.

Chloe reached over and pulled a flower from a vase, which she stuck in her hair. "Her name is Rosa Bud. She's very pretty and feminine and charming. She and Edwin have been engaged since they were children. That's because their parents were good friends and wanted to see them married."

"Chloe, this is a perfect part for you," Sam said.

"I know," Chloe admitted.

"And here is where the plot thickens," Joe said,

making his voice sound just a little villainous. "Secretly, John Jasper is in love with Rosa Bud. He thinks about her all the time. And, because the opium has made him a little crazy, we get the idea that he might do something drastic to get Rosa Bud for himself."

Sam sprang to her feet. "And then the plot thickens even more when Neville and Helena Landless arrive in town."

"Tell us about them," Chloe urged.

Sam picked up a colored scarf that lay on top of Chloe's jacket. "They're brother and sister. They're about the same age as Edwin. They come from Ceylon, which is an island off the south coast of India." Sam wrapped the scarf around her waist as if it were a sash. "Neville is dark and handsome, and very romantic." Then Sam took the scarf from her waist and put it across her face as if it were a veil. "Helena is dark and beautiful, and also very romantic."

Chloe batted her eyes playfully. "Neville instantly falls in love with Rosa Bud."

Sam made the scarf into a sash again, and she stared at Chloe. She deepened her voice and said, "Yes, he most certainly does."

Joe stood up, remembering how the plot grew even thicker. "Then John Jasper gets very sneaky. He arranges things so that Edwin and Neville quarrel about Rosa Bud. Then he makes sure everyone in town knows about the quarrel. Finally, on Christmas Eve, Jasper invites both boys over for dinner and makes peace between them. Afterward, he suggests that Edwin and Neville stroll along the river together. They do."

"Here's where things get really scary," Chloe said, her eyes growing wide. "That night a terrible storm comes to Cloisterham."

"The wind blows wildly all night long," Sam continued, "rattling the shutters and shaking the trees."

"So wild is the wind," Joe added dramatically, "that it rips the hands off the clock on the cathedral tower!"

Wishbone looked from person to person as if he were following every word of the story's plot.

Chloe spoke in a low tone. "But the next morning, everything turns completely calm. Except . . ."

"Except," Sam said quietly, "Edwin Drood has disappeared."

"There's not a sign of him anywhere," whispered Joe. "He seems to have vanished into thin air."

There was a moment of silence as the kids let the spookiness of the event sink in. There was no sound in the room except the ticking of the hallway clock.

Finally, Chloe said, "It's so frustrating, this story— because it ends before any of the answers are revealed."

"Well, that's what we're here for," Sam said, returning to her seat. "We're going to try to figure out what those answers are. All right, let's begin discussing our ideas."

Chloe went to the window and peered outside. "Actually, I think we should wait until we have David with us. He's so incredibly intelligent, I'm sure he'll have great answers."

Sam smiled and rolled her eyes. Joe stifled a laugh. It was now clear to Joe that the main reason Chloe wanted to be there was to see David. However, Joe figured that Chloe did have a point. David would certainly be a big help with the discussion.

"Okay," Joe said. "We'll put the *Drood* discussion on hold until we have David here."

"Great!" Chloe said, going for her jacket. "I need to get going, anyway. The youth group at my church is having a Christmas party at two o'clock. I need some time to fix my hair and stuff. Oh, and if I happen to see David, I'll ask when he might be able to join us for the discussion."

Sam raised her eyebrows. "Joe and I see David all the time. Are you planning to see him before us?"

"You never know," Chloe said, with a shake of her frizzed hair. "Okay, Joe, Sam, thanks so much for having me over. I'll be seeing you again very soon. 'Bye-'bye."

Chloe practically danced her way to the door. When the door closed, Sam showed a smile. "Wow! Chloe is really head over heels about David. I wonder if David has any interest in her. He doesn't seem to, but . . . you never know."

Joe glanced at the clock in the hallway. It was now twelve thirty-five. "I wonder what happened to David. It's just not like him not to show up."

"Sometimes David gets awfully wrapped up in his scientific projects," Sam mentioned. "Do you think he might be working in his garage and he just forgot about the discussion?"

Joe threw some items into his backpack. Then he picked up his jacket. "Let's go next door and check. If he's not there, we can walk around and search for him. Come on, Wishbone."

After Joe and Sam put on their jackets, they and Wishbone walked next door to the Barnes's garage. David spent a lot of time in the garage, working on his various scientific projects. The day was cold enough so that Joe could see puffs of fog drifting out of his mouth as he breathed.

The garage door was closed, so Joe gave it a loud knock. "Hey, David!" he called out. "It's me—Joe! Are you in there?"

There was no answer.

Sam shrugged. "I guess not. If he was in there, he wouldn't ignore you."

Joe, Sam, and Wishbone walked to the front door. There, Sam rang the doorbell several times. There was no answer, either.

Joe stuck his hands in his jacket pockets. "Sam, I'm just a little bit worried."

"Yes, so am I," Sam said, putting a hand on Joe's shoulder.

They stood there a moment, not sure what to do next. Even Wishbone seemed a bit confused.

"I mean, it's probably nothing," Sam said hopefully. "It's probably just a silly misunderstanding."

Joe watched a puff of fog evaporate into the air.

"You know," Joe said, feeling a chill run down his spine, "this is reminding me of *The Mystery of Edwin Drood*. Except, this time, it's not a character in a book who's disappeared. It's our best friend, David."

Chapter Five

The wind whispered eerily through the trees.

"Where could he be? Where could he be? Where could he be?" Joe said the words over and over, as if that would help him find the answer. He glanced at his watch, seeing it was now twelve forty-five.

Sam crouched down to pet Wishbone. "I know David's parents and little sister were going somewhere today. Could David have gone with them?"

"They were going to visit a relative for the day," Joe said, looking at the empty Barnes house. "But David would have called us first if he had decided to go with them. He's very responsible about that sort of thing."

"Then where could he be?" Sam wondered.

An image from the previous night entered Joe's mind—David and Mr. Pruitt standing on the other side of the glass beads in Wanda's house, carrying on a private conversation.

"Last night," Joe mentioned, "I saw Mr. Pruitt take David into the dining room for a private talk. I got the idea that they were up to something—something they didn't want anyone else to know about. Maybe it has to do with where David might be now."

Sam stood up. "Well, why don't we head over to Mr. Pruitt's house? Maybe we'll learn something there. After all, he *is* a teacher."

Wishbone trotted alongside Joe and Sam as the group headed in the direction of Mr. Pruitt's house. Every so often, he sniffed the sidewalk, hoping to pick up a hint of David's scent. So far, he was coming up with nothing.

You know, there are a lot of mysteries going on right now, Wishbone thought. *The ring is missing, the bone is missing, David is missing. I knew there was something going on with all that wind last night. I can't quite put my paw on it, but . . . well, if you ask me, I think the wind blew some kind of mysterious air into town. Yes, it's weird, but that's what I think.*

Wishbone enjoyed sinking his teeth into a good mystery. Besides, with his excellent senses and high level of intelligence, the dog considered himself to be a first-rate detective. Wishbone just hoped that at least some of these mysteries would be solved before the day was over.

The dog felt some of the air's chill easing away. But he noticed a single black cloud floating overhead.

I think that wind also blew a storm this way. I don't know when the storm will arrive, but I know it's coming. We dogs are never wrong about the weather.

Soon, Joe, Sam, and Wishbone arrived at the front porch of Mr. Pruitt's house. Joe lifted his hand to knock at the door. Just before he knocked, however, a strange moaning sound came from inside the house. After a moment, it stopped.

"What was that?" Sam asked.

"Got me," Joe said.

"Got me, too," Wishbone added.

Again, the weird moan sounded. Then it stopped. Joe gave the door a knock.

"Who's there?" Mr. Pruitt's voice called out.

"It's Joe and Sam," Joe called back. "We wanted to talk to you about something."

"Oh, okay," Mr. Pruitt called. "Just give me a minute or two, please."

Joe, Sam, and Wishbone sat down on the steps. "You know what that sound reminded me of?" Joe whispered to Sam.

"A ghost with a really bad head cold?" Wishbone suggested.

"What?" Sam whispered back.

Joe reached inside his backpack and pulled out his copy of *The Mystery of Edwin Drood*. "The weird sounds that John Jasper makes when he's in an opium trance."

"Why did you bring the book along?" Sam asked.

"Well," Joe said, tapping his fingers on the book's worn cover, "I put it in my backpack, thinking we could discuss the book while we were searching for David. But now I'm thinking that the book may even help us find David."

"What do you mean?" Sam said.

"David disappeared just the way Edwin Drood disappeared," Joe explained. "And it happened right at the same time that we're reading *The Mystery of Edwin Drood*. Maybe, in a strange way, the clues in the book can help us find David."

Wishbone felt a chilly breeze ruffle his fur.

Hmm . . . this is very interesting, Wishbone thought, as he stared at the book. *Edwin's disappearance and David's disappearance do seem a lot alike. Maybe that mysterious wind also blew the spirit of Charles Dickens into town. Spirits are supposed to ride the wind sometimes—if there really are spirits.*

"Your book has some cool drawings," Sam said, watching Joe flip through the book. "All the rest of us are just using the modern paperback edition. That doesn't have any pictures."

"Look at this one," Joe said, stopping at a page.

Wishbone and Sam leaned in to see a black-and-white illustration of John Jasper talking to Edwin Drood. Jasper wore a church choir robe. His face was twisted into a tortured expression. A caption showed what he was saying: "No wretched monk who droned his life away in this gloomy place, before me, can have been more tired of it than I am."

"I think Jasper might have murdered Edwin Drood," Joe said. "His boredom drove him to use the opium. The drug made him go a little crazy. Also, he did want Rosa Bud, Edwin's fiancée, all for himself. And I think Jasper might have gotten Neville Landless to quarrel with Edwin so that everyone would think Neville had committed the murder."

Wishbone looked at Joe. "Well, yes, that's a possibility."

"It certainly seems as if Jasper *planned* to murder Edwin," Sam said. "But I'm not so sure that's what actually happened. Someone else might have murdered him. Or he might not have been killed at all."

Wishbone looked at Sam. "Well, yes, those are both possibilities, too."

The door opened, and Mr. Pruitt stood there, wearing slippers, sweat pants, a sweatshirt, and a very elegant silk scarf around his neck. The scarf didn't seem to go with the rest of the outfit. It was the type of thing Wishbone might expect a European prince to wear.

Mr. Pruitt smiled and said, "It's nice to see you. I'm sorry I took so long, but I was . . . uh . . . right in the middle of some messy cleaning. Please come in."

"Thanks," Wishbone said. He led Joe and Sam into the living room. The room was very neat and nicely decorated. Wishbone spotted a few pieces of antique furniture, and several landscape paintings on the wall.

"If you don't mind my asking," Joe said as he and Sam removed their jackets, "what is that you're wearing around your neck?"

"Oh, this?" Mr. Pruitt said, touching the scarf. "It's called an ascot. Sometimes I . . . uh . . . like to dress with a little style around the house."

"Even when you're cleaning?" Sam asked, wrinkling her brow.

"Especially when I'm cleaning," Mr. Pruitt replied.

This made no sense to Wishbone, but he figured he would let the remark go. Everyone sat down, the humans in chairs and Wishbone on the floor.

When Mr. Pruitt crossed his legs, Wishbone saw something rather startling—a shiny silver material peeked out at the bottom of the man's sweat pants. Very casually, Mr. Pruitt reached down and tugged at the sweat pants until the pants covered the shiny material.

What was that? Wishbone thought. *A fancy pair of long underwear? An astronaut's suit?*

Pretending nothing had happened, Mr. Pruitt said pleasantly, "To what do I owe the honor of this visit?"

"By any chance, have you seen David today?" Joe asked.

"Yes. I saw him this morning," Mr. Pruitt replied. "He stopped by my house."

"Oh, really?" Sam said with great interest. "What was he doing here?"

Suddenly, a look of panic crossed Mr. Pruitt's face. "Uh . . . well . . . as a matter of fact . . . he was helping me move some . . . uh . . . foxes."

"Foxes?" Joe said with confusion.

"Why were you moving *foxes?*" Sam said, equally confused.

"Hey, if you're *hunting* foxes," Wishbone said, "you'll need a good hound to help you with the chase."

Mr. Pruitt gave a nervous chuckle. "I . . . uh . . . started to say *furniture,* and then I switched over to *boxes,* and it came out *foxes.* The fact is, David was helping me move both furniture *and* boxes. It was all part of my cleaning process."

Wishbone got the idea that Mr. Pruitt was not telling the complete truth. The dog had a nose for that sort of thing.

"So that's all you and David did?" Joe said. "He just helped you move some foxes . . . uh . . . I mean boxes, and furniture?"

"Uh . . . let me think. . . ." Mr. Pruitt said, running a finger across his lip. "Yes, that's all we did, all right."

He may be doing some cleaning, Wishbone thought, *but he's not coming clean with us.*

Mr. Pruitt shifted in his chair. "Oh, I understand that the eighth-grade English students are reading *The Mystery of Edwin Drood.* How do you like it?"

"Joe and I both think it's really interesting," Sam answered.

"Isn't Dickens a wonderful writer?" Mr. Pruitt said, fiddling with his ascot. "When it comes to writing a big, thick, juicy stew of a novel, Charles Dickens is about the best. He wrote so many wonderful works: *A Christmas Carol, David Copperfield, Great Expectations, A Tale of Two Cities, The Old Curiosity Shop.*"

Wishbone could see that Mr. Pruitt was trying very hard to keep the discussion away from the subject of David.

"I'd like to read some more of his books," Joe said.

"Oh, you should," Mr. Pruitt said with enthusiasm. "All of his stories have these wonderful plots that twist and turn like the back alleys of old London. And he created such a fascinating group of characters: Smike, Squeers, Scrooge, Pip, Tiny Tim, Little Nell."

"Yes," Joe said, "he creates great char——"

Mr. Pruitt continued. "Mr. Pickwick, Mr. Bucket, Mr. Bumble, Miss Havisham, Mrs. Jellyby, Madame De Farge."

"I know," Joe said, "but—"

"And, oh, yes," Mr. Pruitt added, "let's not forget the Artful Dodger."

"And let's not forget Bull's-eye," Wishbone added. "He's the dog in *Oliver Twist*. Not a very nice dog, though."

Joe held up a hand as if he were a traffic cop. "Mr. Pruitt, we'd love to sit around and discuss Dickens with you someday. But right now, you see, we really need to find David."

Mr. Pruitt gave a serious nod. "I see. Well, David came here around ten, and he left here around eleven. I have no idea where he was headed. He didn't say."

"Okay, thanks," Sam said, standing up. "We're sorry to have bothered you."

"Oh, nonsense! Think nothing of it," Mr. Pruitt said with a wave of his hand. "That's the good thing about dressing with style around the house. You're always ready when guests drop by."

Joe and Sam picked up their jackets and got ready to leave. Mr. Pruitt showed them to the door.

"Good luck with the cleaning," Wishbone told Mr. Pruitt.

After Mr. Pruitt shut the door, Joe, Sam, and Wishbone headed for the street. Only when they were passing by the neighboring house did Joe speak. "Tell me if I'm wrong, but wasn't Mr. Pruitt acting really odd?"

"He was definitely acting odd," Sam agreed. "And I thought that scarf was weird, too—especially if he was just cleaning the house."

"Maybe Mr. Pruitt has some dark secret," Joe said after taking a few steps. "You know, like John Jasper does."

"Dark secret?" Wishbone said with alarm. "Mr. Pruitt is the most mild-mannered man I know."

"What sort of dark secret?" Sam asked.

"It wouldn't be anything really dark," Joe said. "Nothing like, say, smoking opium or robbing banks or cheating on his taxes. But it seems that he is up to something he doesn't want us to know about. I know he would never put David in any danger, but maybe his secret has something to do with David's disappearance."

Sam considered that idea for a moment. "I don't know, Joe. Maybe you're taking this Edwin Drood connection too far. I'm still hoping there's a very simple explanation for all this. Right now, let's head downtown and see if we can find David around there."

"Good idea," Wishbone said eagerly. "Let's see what's going down downtown."

Chapter Six

Downtown Oakdale was alive with a sense of holiday hustle-and-bustle. People were coming and going, many of them carrying shopping bags. And most folks seemed even friendlier than usual. Everyone was getting caught up in the holiday spirit.

As Joe walked, he kept watching for David. He figured there was a good chance his friend would be around somewhere nearby. Oakdale was not a large town. Most of its stores and businesses were located right in the downtown area.

Joe noticed the large clock that sat on top of the town hall building. It was one-thirty.

Then Joe saw Wanda coming toward him. Her face was partly hidden by a very large box. "Hi, Miss Gilmore," Joe greeted her. "Here, let me help you with that box."

"Oh, hi, Joe, Sam," Wanda said as she gave Joe the box. For some reason, Wanda shot Wishbone an irritated look. Then she began to walk alongside the kids. "I just picked that box up at the costume shop. It's the Santa Claus outfit for Bob Pruitt to wear at the tree-lighting ceremony."

"Have you seen David today?" Sam asked Wanda.

"No, I haven't," Wanda replied. "Why?"

52

"Because we're trying to locate him," Sam told her. "If you happen to see him, please tell him that."

"I certainly will," Wanda said, stopping beside her white convertible, which was parked on the street. Wanda opened the car door, and Joe put the box inside. "Thanks," Wanda told Joe. "Now I just need to go to the grocery store. Then I'll be done with my errands for the day. Of course, then I have to track down some elves, but that's another story."

As Wanda headed toward the grocery store, Joe and Sam sat on the bench in front of the post office. Wishbone made himself comfortable on the sidewalk. Joe glanced here and there, hoping that he might spot David. Sam absently pulled her jacket zipper up and down. She seemed to be deep in thought.

Eventually, Sam said, "Here's an idea. You saw how Chloe attached herself to David last night." Sam explained, "And you know how uncomfortable David gets in these types of situations. I'm thinking maybe David didn't show up just because he didn't want to deal with Chloe."

Joe tapped his fingers on his backpack, thinking about Sam's idea. He knew that David was a little shy, especially when it came to dealing with members of the opposite sex. "Yes, that's possible. Only—"

"Only what?"

"Even if David wanted to stay away because of Chloe, I still can't see him doing that without telling us. He would just have called me and said, 'Joe, I can't deal with Chloe, so I think I'll skip the meeting.'"

"You're right," Sam agreed. "Okay, forget that theory. But, listen, I just thought of another one. David told me he felt badly about you losing your father's ring. Maybe he's out looking for it. Maybe he didn't call because he wanted to surprise you if he actually was able to find it."

"It still doesn't make sense," Joe said. "Even if that

was David's plan, he still would have called to say he wasn't coming. He might have given a phony reason why he wasn't coming, but he would have called. Besides, David and I looked all over the place for that ring."

"I know. He told me the same thing. I offered to help him look, but he said there was no point. So I guess we can also file away the ring theory."

Joe looked up, as if searching the air for the correct explanation. "David is very responsible. He wouldn't leave us hanging like this unless . . . I don't know . . . unless it was some really big reason."

"Let's go into some of the stores," Sam suggested. "Who knows? Maybe someone there will have seen David today."

"Good idea," Joe said as he stood up. "Wishbone, why don't you wait right here for us? We'll just be a few minutes. If you see David, give a bark."

Sam scratched the top of Wishbone's head. "I don't know if he understands you, but sometimes I'm almost sure he does."

Sam and Joe walked down the street.

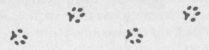

"Of course I understand you," Wishbone called to the kids. "What do you think, I'm hard of hearing? I've got the finest hearing in the world. Oh, guys, while you're up, maybe you can bring me something to eat. It's way past my lunch hour, and all this detective work is making me extra hungry!"

Just then, Wishbone saw Sparkey, his golden retriever friend, wandering down the street. Looking here and there for something interesting to sniff or chew, Sparkey came to one of the public trash containers. The large dog raised himself up and put his front paws on the top of the container to take a look inside.

"Wow! Sparkey sure has a healthy appetite," Wishbone said to himself. "Myself, I don't eat garbage even when I'm really desperately hungry. But, Sparkey, he doesn't care what it is or who it belongs to—"

Suddenly, Wishbone remembered the pretzel-shaped rawhide bone—the one that had mysteriously disappeared. Wishbone had to find it and put it back in its proper place before Ellen came home that evening.

Could Sparkey have stolen the bone? Wishbone wondered.

Wishbone thought back to that morning, shortly before the hour of noon. He had been gnawing on the rawhide bone in Wanda's backyard. Sparkey came over and eyed the bone hungrily. Then he and Sparkey had gone on their cat chase. Wanda was there, too, either cheering the dogs on or yelling at them about something—Wishbone couldn't remember which. After the chase was over, Wishbone said good-bye to Sparkey and went to greet Joe. At that point, Wishbone remembered the bone and ran back to fetch it in Wanda's backyard. But the bone was gone.

Wishbone realized that Sparkey could have stolen the bone while he was off greeting Joe.

I told Sparkey he couldn't have the bone, Wishbone reasoned. *And Sparkey's a friend. But . . . how good a friend? That's the big question.*

Wishbone looked at Sparkey, who was still examining the contents of the trash barrel. Wishbone knew he had to figure out who or what had taken the bone. Only then could he figure out how to get the bone back.

Sparkey turned his head. He seemed to have heard the mail carrier, Mr. Bloodgood. The man was coming down the street, pushing his mail cart.

I know what Sparkey's thinking—treat!

Mr. Bloodgood was a solidly built fellow with

longish black hair. All the local dogs knew that he carried a supply of doggie treats, which he delivered on a daily basis. The man also delivered the mail, but that wasn't nearly as important a job.

Sparkey left the trash barrel and trotted toward Mr. Bloodgood. Wishbone saw an opportunity to test Sparkey's friendship. "Hey, Sparkey!" he barked out.

Sparkey stopped and turned to look at Wishbone. The golden retriever was now standing halfway between Wishbone and the approaching mail carrier.

"Could you come over here for a second?" Wishbone called. "I need to talk to you. Dog to dog. At once. It's a matter of extreme importance!"

Sparkey stared at Wishbone blankly.

Now, let's see if he comes to me, or if he goes for the treat. We'll see how true a friend he is.

Hearing the wheels of the mail cart coming closer, Sparkey turned his head in that direction. He stared at the mail carrier. Then he turned back to Wishbone. Sparkey seemed to be wrestling with a difficult decision. After a moment, Sparkey raced straight for the mail carrier.

Aha! Maybe he's not such a good friend after all!

Wishbone watched Sparkey come up alongside Mr. Bloodgood. He eagerly accepted a treat from the mail carrier's hand.

Yes, indeed, my old friend Sparkey must have stolen my bone. But hold on, I don't know that for certain. Remember, a dog is innocent until proven guilty. I need solid proof. Wait! That bone had a very beefy flavor. If Sparkey has had that thing in his mouth anytime today, I'll be able to pick up the scent instantly. My nose is never wrong.

Wishbone trotted over to Sparkey. He was now following at the mail carrier's heels, probably hoping to receive a second treat. Unfortunately, the mail carrier had a rule of "one treat per dog per day." Wishbone figured that was a government regulation.

As Wishbone approached, Mr. Bloodgood stopped his cart. "Well, hello, there, Wishbone. How goes it?"

"Be right with you," Wishbone told Mr. Bloodgood.

Sparkey leaned down to give Wishbone a sniff. Wishbone took a good sniff of his own, right in the area of Sparkey's mouth. Wishbone picked up all sorts of scents on Sparkey's breath. There was one scent he did *not* detect—rawhide bone with beef flavoring.

"Sparkey," Wishbone said, "this court now declares you to be innocent. There is no way you stole that bone." Wishbone looked over at Mr. Bloodgood. "Okay, sir, I will take my treat now."

Mr. Bloodgood handed Wishbone a small dog treat. The dog ate it immediately. Just as Wishbone was licking his chops, Joe and Sam came over.

"Hi, kids," Mr. Bloodgood greeted them. "How's it going this fine winter day?"

"It's going okay, I guess," Joe replied. "But have you seen David anywhere? We're having some trouble finding him."

"No," Mr. Bloodgood said. "Come to think of it, I haven't seen David at all today."

"Well, thanks," Sam said. "Okay, Joe, let's try looking in some more stores."

"I see you didn't get me anything to eat," Wishbone scolded the kids. "This time I'd better come with you."

Wishbone trotted after Joe and Sam.

Joe entered the Oakdale Attic. Wishbone and Sam were right behind him. It was a small shop filled with all sorts of interesting antique items—framed mirrors, used books, artwork, old clothing, and antique jewelry. Joe watched Wishbone shopping around the store for any food crumbs that might have fallen on the floor. Several customers were also browsing through the shop.

Joe went up to a young lady at the main counter. "Hi, Mary. By any chance, have you seen David today?"

Mary shook her head. "Sorry, Joe, don't believe I have. . . . That was some terrible wind that we had last night, wasn't it?"

"Yes, it was," Joe replied.

Sam nudged Joe. "Look, there's Mrs. Hernandez's niece, Lola."

Hearing her name, Lola turned around. She was standing by a counter that contained secondhand purses. The girl seemed very surprised to see Joe and Sam, who walked over to her.

"Hi, Lola," Joe said with a friendly smile. "How are you doing?"

Lola gave a toss of her glossy black hair. "Oh, I suppose I'm doing okay."

"Are you shopping for a present?" Sam asked, trying to be friendly.

"Yes, I am," Lola replied. Suddenly, she turned around and began to sort through the purses sitting on another counter. Joe got the feeling that the girl was angry about something.

"For your mother?" Sam asked.

"Yes, my mother," Lola said, as she held up a purse.

"I like that one a lot," Sam said. "It looks like genuine leather."

Lola dropped that purse and picked up another. "Yes, it looks like genuine leather. They all do. But are they? That's the problem with these secondhand stores. You never know if you're getting the real thing, or a phony. So you know what I'm going to do? I'm going to look somewhere else!"

Lola tossed the purse on the counter. Then, without another word, she walked out of the store.

Joe turned to Sam. "What was that all about?"

"I don't know," Sam said with a shrug. "She seemed angry at us for some reason. Really angry. That's very odd. She seemed so friendly when we first met her."

Joe and Sam sat in two antique chairs that were near the purses. When Wishbone trotted over, Sam pulled the dog into her lap.

"Remember last night?" Sam said, staring at the door through which Lola had just left. "Remember how Luis thought David was insulting him? Maybe Lola also thought David was insulting him. Maybe they're both still angry about that. Maybe they're also angry at us because we're friends with David."

"That could be it," Joe said thoughtfully. "Sometimes brothers and sisters stick together on things like that. In *The Mystery of Edwin Drood,* when everyone thinks Neville Landless has murdered Edwin, his sister, Helena, is one of the only people who sticks up for him."

"There you go with that *Edwin Drood* connection again," Sam said, smiling.

"I know," Joe said, reaching inside his backpack. "I can't seem to get the story out of my head."

Joe pulled out the book and thumbed through it again. He stopped at an illustration of Helena Landless. She was staring at someone, with her dark, Gypsy-like features and a fierce gleam in her eyes. A caption showed what Helena was saying: "I fear you under no circumstances."

"I really like those drawings," Sam said, as she and Wishbone both leaned in to get a better look. "Joe, is there a picture of Rosa Bud in there? I'm curious to see what she looks like."

Joe flipped through the book and found another illustration. This one showed Rosa Bud, a pretty, young girl with her hair styled in curls. She was looking at Edwin Drood with love. He was glancing down, embarrassed. A caption showed what Rosa was saying: "I got the gloves last evening, Eddy, and I like them very much. They are beauties."

Sam studied the picture for a few moments. Then her hazel eyes lit up, as if she were making a sudden discovery. "You're right, Joe. Looking at this book has given me an idea about why David might have skipped our meeting today. Thinking about the relationship between Rosa Bud and Edwin helped me get the idea."

"Well, what's your idea?" Joe asked eagerly.

"Brace yourself."

"Brace myself? Why?"

Sam gave a cautious look. "Because you may find it a little scary."

Wishbone's ears shot up straight.

Chapter Seven

"Scary?" Wishbone repeated with concern. "Sam, what are you talking about?"

"Tell me," Joe told Sam. "I can take it. At least I think I can."

Sam glanced at a nearby customer in the shop. Then she lowered her voice. "Okay, here it goes. Maybe David didn't show up today not because he was running away from Chloe—but because he *likes* her."

There was a long pause.

Finally, Joe said, "You mean he *really* likes her?"

"Yes, but keep your voice down," Sam warned.

Wishbone twitched his whiskers. "No, Sam, you've got it all wrong. Chloe isn't David's type. She's too . . . too . . . well, *too something.*"

"Look, even if that's true," Joe said in a low voice, "why would that make David not come to our discussion session?"

"Yeah, why?" Wishbone added.

"Here's why," Sam said calmly. "If David *does* like Chloe, who are the last two people he would want to know about it?

Joe thought a moment. "You and I. Because he would think that we would think that Chloe is too . . . too . . . much."

"Yeah, too much," Wishbone said, jumping from Sam's lap into Joe's lap. "That's the word."

"Exactly," Sam said, pointing at Joe. "And maybe David thought we would catch on to him if we spent any more time with him and Chloe in the same room together. As we both know, David isn't very good at keeping things from us."

"But I was watching David last night," Joe argued. "He seemed embarrassed around Chloe."

"True," Sam said. "But why was he embarrassed? Was it because he didn't like Chloe hanging all over him? Or was it because he didn't want anyone to know he *didn't mind* Chloe hanging all over him? Remember, it was David who invited Chloe over to Miss Gilmore's house. And it was David who invited her to our discussion group."

Joe rubbed his chin in thought. Then he said only, "Hmm . . ."

"Hmm is right," Wishbone agreed. "Yep, there was definitely something in that wind."

"And maybe," Sam continued, "David was so afraid of us finding out about this that he didn't even want to call you to say he wouldn't be coming to the book discussion."

Joe began to rub his forehead. Wishbone could see that Joe was as confused by this information as he was.

"Even if this is true," Joe told Sam, "and I'm not saying it is, then where is David right now?"

"Yeah, where is he right now?" Wishbone asked.

"Earlier at your house," Sam explained, "I remember that Chloe said she might be seeing David later in the day. I also remember that she said her youth group at the church was having a party at two o'clock this afternoon. I'm thinking maybe David was planning to go to the party—as Chloe's guest."

Wishbone shifted in Joe's lap. "Oh, no, this is getting scarier by the second."

Joe checked his watch. "Personally, I doubt that David is at that party. But I'd sure like to know *where* he is. It's a little after two now. Maybe we should stop by the party just to make sure he's not there."

"Good idea," Wishbone said, giving Joe a quick lick. "I wonder what kind of food they're serving. That treat I had before really got my appetite going."

"It's not so simple," Sam pointed out. "If David *is* at that party, he certainly doesn't want us to know about it. And he would be pretty embarrassed if he saw us show up there."

Wishbone pawed at Joe's chest. "Oh, I'll go. I'll keep my head down so no one will recognize me. And while I'm there, maybe I'll grab a snack."

"I wonder if one of us could go in disguise," Joe said, still rubbing his chin.

"Good thinking!" Wishbone exclaimed. "I'll go disguised as an English sheepdog!"

"A disguise?" Sam said with a chuckle. "You mean, kind of like Dick Datchery?"

Wishbone knew that Dick Datchery was a character in *The Mystery of Edwin Drood*. He showed up in Cloisterham after Edwin's disappearance. He had supposedly gone there to solve the mystery of what happened to Edwin. He had a white beard, but very dark eyebrows, which meant he was really someone in disguise. Part of the school assignment was to figure out the true identity of Dick Datchery.

"I've got a great idea!" Joe announced.

"Shh!" Sam urged. "Keep your voice down."

"It's another idea inspired by *The Mystery of Edwin Drood*," Joe whispered. "Remember how Dick Datchery used a white beard for a disguise? Well, maybe I could do the same thing."

"What are you talking about?" Sam and Wishbone whispered together.

"You know—the Santa Claus costume!" Joe cried out. "Come on!"

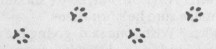

Joe stared in the mirror at Santa Claus, which was really himself. He was standing in the men's rest room of the church. He was wearing a red-velvet coat, a shiny black belt, a red cap, a white wig, and a fluffy white beard. Joe had left the Santa pants and boots outside the church with Sam. He figured he didn't need them.

A short while ago, Joe and Sam had found Wanda leaving the grocery store. She agreed to let them borrow the costume, as long as they took it to Mr. Pruitt's house for him when they were done with it.

I'm not the most convincing Santa Claus, Joe thought as he adjusted the beard. *But at least I won't be recognized.*

Joe left the rest room and walked down the hallway of the church. He was glad to see there was no one around. Joe turned a corner. Soon his ears picked up the easily recognizable sound of chattering, laughing girls. Joe figured that was the party. He didn't hear any boys talking, but he knew that boys were sometimes quieter than girls in these social situations.

Could David really be at the party? Joe wondered.

Joe felt a bead of sweat form on his forehead. He wasn't sure if it was caused by the heavy costume or his nervousness. Joe had girls as friends, and he had even *liked* a few. However, they did make him feel uneasy sometimes, especially away from a school function.

With every step, the chattering and laughing grew louder. The sounds were pretty loud by the time Joe arrived at the open door of the party room. Joe didn't plan to enter. He was just going to peek inside and see for himself whether or not David was there.

Keeping against the wall, Joe eased his white-haired head into the doorway. He saw girls, girls, and more girls. There were about two dozen of them, eating cookies, drinking punch, and, most of all, chattering and laughing. Chloe Devine was present. Joe knew most of the other girls, as well. But there was not a single boy in the room.

Mission accomplished, Joe thought. *David is not here.*

Joe continued to watch for a few moments. Soon Chloe raised a hand and called out cheerfully, "Everyone, I have an announcement to make."

"Did you finally get David Barnes to ask you to go steady?" one of the girls asked.

"She wishes!" another girl teased.

This was followed by giggles.

"No, it's not that," Chloe said, fingering a lock of her frizzy hair. "But I need everyone to gather around me. This is top-secret information. What I am about to say cannot go outside this room."

Yeah, right, Joe thought. *There's a good chance of that.*

Joe was about to leave. Suddenly, he realized this information might possibly have something to do with David. He figured he should listen in, just in case it did.

The girls gathered around Chloe. She began to speak in a whisper. She seemed to be repeating the fact that this was top-secret information, but Joe had difficulty making out the exact words. He needed to get closer. Figuring the girls were too focused on Chloe to notice him, Joe took a cautious step into the room.

Chloe continued to talk, but Joe still had trouble making out the words. Very quietly, he inched his way farther into the room.

". . . and so," Chloe was whispering, "are most of

you going to the tree-lighting ceremony on Friday night?"

There were nods and whispers of "yes."

"Well, a little while ago," Chloe went on, "I got a call from Mr. Pruitt. You know, he's the sixth-grade English teacher at Sequoyah. He told me there's going to be a very special event at the tree-lighting ceremony. He wanted me to get a bunch of my friends to help out. When the right time comes, he wants us to jump up and down and scream as if we're seeing the greatest thing."

"What's this very special event?" a girl asked.

"He wouldn't tell me," Chloe replied, "but he said it would come right after he read a certain poem. He also said we'd know what the special thing was when we saw it. And remember, even though we don't know exactly what it is, we have to keep what we do know totally and completely secret."

Joe found this information interesting. Now he knew for sure that Mr. Pruitt was up to something of a secret nature. He wondered what it was, and if it could somehow have something to do with David's disappearance.

Joe was so busy with his wondering that he didn't notice one of the girls turning around to see him. The girl pointed right at Joe and squealed, "Hey! Look, everybody! It's Santa Claus!"

Joe froze as every pair of female eyes focused in his direction. Even though David was not there, Joe wanted to keep his identity a secret. If the girls figured out that Joe was there, there was no telling what they might think.

"Yo-ho-ho-ho!" Joe said with a jolly laugh. He gave a friendly wave and then headed for the door.

A few of the girls flew toward the door, cutting off Joe's escape route. One of them said, "What's your rush, Santa? You've still got plenty of time until Christmas Eve arrives."

A ripple of giggles went around. Joe heard Chloe's

bird-chirping laugh. The girls by the door walked toward Joe, forcing him all the way to the center of the room. Before Joe knew it, he was surrounded by every girl at the party.

"Should we tell you what we want for Christmas?" one of the girls asked.

Joe knew it was important to disguise his voice. Making it as deep as possible, he said, "Not right now, girls."

Joe made another move for the door. It was clear, though, that he would not get through the circle of girls without a bit of a struggle.

Chloe fixed her blue eyes mischievously on Joe. "I don't think this is the real Santa. I think it's just a boy from school."

Joe felt sweat dripping down his face. "Yo-ho-ho! I tell you, 'tis I, the one and only Santa Claus."

"If you're Santa Claus, then why are you wearing jeans instead of your Santa pants?" a girl asked.

"My Santa pants are at the cleaner's," Joe answered. "I spilled some . . . uh . . . snow on them."

The girls began an excited discussion of the situation.

"This is definitely just a boy our own age."

"But why would a boy want to come to our party?"

"An all-girls' party."

"I know."

"Me, too."

"Maybe he just wants to be around a bunch of girls!"

"Isn't that sweet?"

"That is so sweet."

"And very romantic."

"*Sooo* romantic."

"We have to find what boy has such a romantic nature. Then we can tell the whole school about it!"

By this time, Joe felt rivers of sweat flowing down his face and inside his Santa costume. He got the feeling the girls were teasing him. All the same, even in a teasing way, he didn't want this incident getting around school.

"Well, I'd better be going," Joe said in his best Santa voice. "I think I hear Rudolph calling."

Joe made another move for the door, but the girls were not about to move out of the way. In fact, they seemed to be closing in on him. All the while, the girls continued to discuss the situation.

"Who do you suppose it is?"

"I think it's Kevin Ryan."

"I think it's Johnny Brodman."

I don't know *who* it is, but I'm totally determined to find out."

"So am I."

"It's easy enough to do. All we have to do is pull off his beard."

"Let's go!" Chloe ordered.

Joe knew there was only one thing left to do—run for his life!

Acting as if he were on the football field, Joe picked out a space between two of his opponents and charged. A tangle of hands grabbed at him. One of them pulled off the beard. However, Joe was already out the door. He was pretty sure no one had caught even a glimpse of his face.

The beardless Joe dashed his fastest down the church hallway, but he was far from free. He heard what sounded like a hundred female feet chasing after him.

Chapter Eight

Just as a minister opened the door of the church, Wishbone dashed inside and raced down the hallway. Although Sam had tried to stop the dog, he was determined to visit the party and find something to satisfy his fierce hunger.

As Wishbone ran, he heard what sounded like a stampede of wild animals. Soon, a boy wearing part of a Santa Claus costume came tearing around a corner, followed by a group of highly excited girls.

"Joe!" Wishbone called as he ran up to meet his best buddy. "What's going on here?"

"Out of my way, strange dog!" Joe yelled without stopping. "Whoever you are!"

Wishbone turned to watch Joe race away. *Why was Joe pretending he didn't know me? And why was he using that phony voice? And why did he look so frightened? Those girls certainly can't do him much harm. I'll investigate this as soon as—*

The next second, Wishbone was almost flattened by the charging herd of girls. The dog scurried out of the way.

After the last girl had gone by, Wishbone went back to his food mission, soon finding the party room. The party seemed to have disappeared, but there was a tempting assortment of cookies left on a long table. Unfortunately, Wishbone was unable to find a way to reach the cookies.

Oh, well, Wishbone thought with disappointment, *that's the way the cookie crumbles.* As the dog headed for the door, he spotted a white beard lying on the floor.

Joe shouldn't be so careless with this thing, Wishbone thought, as he grabbed the beard in his mouth. Wishbone ran down the hallway and left through the church door just as the group of girls was walking back inside.

Wishbone heard one of the girls say in frustration, "I just don't know where he went."

I do, Wishbone thought, as he lowered his nose to the ground. He followed Joe's scent until he found his buddy hiding in a bunch of bushes clear on the other side of the church building. Wishbone entered the bushes, seeing that Joe was breathing hard, with sweat pouring down his face.

"Way to go, Wishbone!" Joe said, taking the beard from the dog's mouth. "I was wondering how I would get this thing back."

"You're welcome," Wishbone replied. "Now, could you tell me what we're doing in these bushes?"

After a cautious peek through the bushes, Joe crawled out. As soon as Wishbone stepped out, he saw Sam run over with a box and Joe's jacket and backpack in her arms—and a very confused look on her face.

"I was waiting right outside the church for you," Sam told Joe. "But then you didn't come. And then Wishbone got away from me. What's going on here?"

As Joe took off the Santa costume and put it back into the box, he explained his run-in with the girls at the party. Sam and Wishbone both had a good laugh when they heard the story. Soon, the trio was on its way.

"It's getting close to three," Joe said, checking his watch. "And we still have no answers about David. I say we pay Mr. Pruitt another visit. Now we know for sure he's up to something, and maybe it's related to what David is doing."

It seems that nice Mr. Pruitt does have a dark secret, Wishbone thought as he walked. *Yep, that wind really blew some major strangeness into town.*

Suddenly, Wishbone lifted his ears. He detected a strange sound. After a moment, he realized it was the same ghostly moaning he had heard at Mr. Pruitt's house earlier in the day. Wishbone scampered toward the sound. Soon he was coming toward the beige building that was Sequoyah Middle School.

"Wishbone, come back!" Joe called as he and Sam ran after the dog.

"Wait," Sam said, slowing down as she neared the school. "Do you hear that sound?"

"It's Mr. Pruitt," Wishbone told his friends.

"That's the same sound we heard at Mr. Pruitt's house," Joe said, putting a hand to his ear. "Mr. Pruitt must be in the school."

Wishbone gave a sigh. "I just told you that."

Joe went to the front door of the school and pushed. The door was unlocked. An empty hallway stretched before Wishbone and his friends. Out of the silence drifted the weird moaning sound. It came, then went, just as it had at Mr. Pruitt's house. Wishbone, Joe, and Sam followed the sound, which soon led them to the door of the auditorium. Joe tried the door, but this one was locked.

"I know another way in," Joe whispered. He quickly led Sam and Wishbone down the hall, up a flight of steps, then through another door. This brought the group to the back of the auditorium's balcony. After Joe and Sam crouched down, the kids and Wishbone crept quietly toward the front of the balcony. All three took a peek over the railing.

Wishbone's lower jaw dropped open with shock. The famous rock-and-roll singer Elvis Presley was standing on the stage!

Then Wishbone realized it wasn't the real Elvis Presley, who had actually been dead for a number of years. It was Mr. Pruitt—dressed as Elvis Presley. The man wore a glittery silver jumpsuit with a turned-up collar and a wig made of black hair.

Wishbone glanced at Joe and Sam. Both of them were staring openmouthed at the stage.

Mr. Pruitt opened his mouth and released a long moaning sound. Wishbone now understood that the sound was a kind of warm-up for the man's voice. Then Mr. Pruitt, who still hadn't noticed the visitors, tapped his foot, saying, "A-one, and a-two, and a-three, and a . . ."

At that point, even though there was no music, Mr. Pruitt began to sing into a microphone that he held. His voice took on the deep tones and thick Southern drawl of Elvis Presley. The song had a strong rock-and-roll beat.

Wishbone soon realized, however, that it was really a well-known Christmas carol. Mr. Pruitt was singing:

> *Deck the halls with boughs of holly,*
> *Fa-la-la-la-la-la-la-la-la.*

On each "la," mild-mannered Mr. Pruitt gave a wild wiggle of his hips. As Wishbone watched, he remembered that he had seen Mr. Pruitt do the Elvis act once before. About two years ago, to everyone's amazement, the teacher had played Elvis in a local talent show.

Mr. Pruitt kept singing and wiggling:

> *'Tis the season to be jolly,*
> *Fa-la-la-la-la-la-la-la-la.*

With each note, Mr. Pruitt's performance grew louder and more dramatic. On some of the words, he even curled up his lips as Elvis used to do. Now that Wishbone had overcome his shock, he was fighting the desire to laugh. Mr. Pruitt wasn't a bad Elvis, but there was something very comical about the whole situation. Wishbone looked next to him and noticed that Joe and Sam were also trying hard to hold back their laughter.

Mr. Pruitt let loose with:

> *Don we now our gay apparel,*
> *Fa-la-la-la-la-la-la-la-la!*

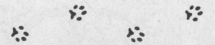

Joe struggled with all his might not to laugh. He bit on his lower lip, but he felt his eyes growing wider and wider, as if they would soon pop out of his head. Finally, a loud gurgle sounded deep in Joe's throat.

Immediately, Mr. Pruitt stopped singing. He looked around the auditorium and called out, "Is somebody in here?"

A tense moment passed.

Joe stood up. "It's me—Joe Talbot."

Sam stood up. "And me—Sam Kepler."

Joe noticed Wishbone lifting a paw for some reason.

Mr. Pruitt's face turned beet-red with embarrassment. "Oh, hi, kids. I was just . . . uh . . . well . . . I was just . . . uh . . ."

Sam finished the sentence. "Pretending you were Elvis Presley."

Joe began to chuckle. Sam elbowed him, warning him not to laugh at Mr. Pruitt.

"As a matter of fact, that's right," Mr. Pruitt admitted. "But I didn't expect anyone to see me in here today. I thought the door was locked."

"We're really sorry," Joe said. "We probably shouldn't have sneaked in here, but, well . . ."

Joe and Sam told Mr. Pruitt the story of their day up to that point.

"I see," Mr. Pruitt said when the explanation was done. "Under the circumstances, I forgive you for sneaking in. I see it was all in the interest of finding David."

"That's right," Sam said. "And we won't tell anybody what we saw in here. We promise."

Mr. Pruitt pulled off his Elvis wig. "I'll explain. Last night, Miss Gilmore said she wanted to do something different and exciting for this year's tree-lighting ceremony. And she's right. The Santa act is nice, but I do that every year. So I sat there, trying to come up with an unusual idea. In the meantime, she was going on and on about how she wanted to get some elves for the ceremony. Suddenly, the talk of elves got me thinking about my Elvis act."

"I remember that you performed as Elvis once a

couple of years ago," Sam said, a grin creeping across her face. "You were good."

"Thanks," Mr. Pruitt said, as he pulled a stray thread off his shiny jumpsuit. "Well, I decided to dig up my Elvis act for the tree-lighting ceremony. As soon as I got the idea, I took David into the dining room because I wanted him to help me out with the sound and lighting. Then we met this morning to discuss the details. That's what we were really doing—not moving furniture and boxes. But, you see, I wanted to keep the whole plan a secret."

"And that moaning sound we heard was your voice warm-up," Joe guessed.

"And when we came to your house, you were trying on the outfit," Sam added. "You threw some clothes over it and put on the ascot so we wouldn't see the collar."

"Correct on all accounts," Mr. Pruitt said with a nod.

"But you're going to be playing Santa," Sam pointed out. "How can you be *both* Santa and Elvis?"

"Oh, you'll see," Mr. Pruitt said with a mischievous smile. "I just hope I don't look too big in this costume. But, then, Elvis was rather big in his later years."

Joe leaned on the balcony railing. "One more thing. Do you have any idea where David might be right now?"

Mr. Pruitt shrugged. "No, I really don't."

"Could he be out collecting sound and lighting equipment for your act?" Sam asked.

Mr. Pruitt thought for a moment. "I don't think so. David told me all the equipment he needed was right here at the school. I was going to meet him here tomorrow and let him into the backstage storage room."

"And so the mystery continues," Joe said, mostly to himself.

"Listen, kids," Mr. Pruitt said gently, "I'm sure David is just fine. He's not the kind of boy to be getting himself into a messy situation. And speaking of a mess, I need to get home to do some cleaning for real. I have some guests coming for dinner tonight."

"Oh, by the way," Joe said, picking up the box, "we have your Santa Claus outfit. We'll bring it down to you."

Joe, Sam, and Wishbone climbed down a set of steps that took them to the auditorium's main level. Joe and Sam sat in the front row, and Sam pulled Wishbone into her lap. Mr. Pruitt began to put his sweat pants and sweatshirt on over his Elvis outfit. He asked, "So, have you kids figured out *The Mystery of Edwin Drood* yet?"

"No, but we're working on it," Joe replied.

"In a way," Mr. Pruitt mentioned, "that novel is the greatest mystery story in all of literature."

"You mean because the mystery can never be solved?" Sam said, scratching Wishbone between his ears.

Mr. Pruitt nodded. "That's right. And, apparently, the book caused a lot of trouble in Dickens's time."

"Why is that?" Joe asked.

"You see," Mr. Pruitt said, "all of Dickens's books came out first in serial form. Do you know what that is?"

"Yes, we learned about that in class," Sam said. "It means the book comes out in one piece at a time—once a month or once a week, or whatever. It's sort of like watching a television series."

"Well, Dickens was very popular in his day," Mr. Pruitt explained. "So thousands of people were reading the *Drood* segments as soon as they came out. Then, suddenly, right smack in the middle of writing the book, Dickens died—while having dinner, I think. His readers were in shock. Not only were they sorry to lose England's greatest author, but they were left hanging in the middle of the story."

Sam shook her head with disbelief. "It's just so weird that no one knows the real ending to this book. Mr. Pruitt, do you know if Dickens at least left behind some notes that hinted where the story was going? Or did he tell anyone how the story was going to come out?"

Joe smiled, realizing Sam was becoming almost as haunted by the story as he already was.

Mr. Pruitt sat on the edge of the stage as he changed his sparkling Elvis shoes for his regular shoes. "Dickens did leave some notes, but they're not very helpful. And, no, it seems that he didn't tell a soul about the book's outcome. He kept it a closely guarded secret. Just a few months before his death, however, Dickens met with Queen Victoria, who was the queen of England. Some people think that Dickens was prepared to tell her, and her alone, what the outcome of the book was. But, unfortunately, she never asked him to."

"Hmm . . ." Joe said, finding all this fascinating. "Our teacher told us that over the years a lot of people have tried to figure out the ending. A few modern authors even wrote their own endings to the book."

Sam grabbed Joe's arm. "Oh, and we also learned that some spiritual mediums have tried to get in touch with the ghost of Charles Dickens. That way, *he* could reveal the ending himself. I doubt any of them got hold of him, though."

Joe noticed that Wishbone was suddenly looking around the auditorium. It almost seemed as if the dog was searching for the spirit of Charles Dickens.

"There was even a Broadway musical based on the book," Mr. Pruitt told the kids. "During the performance, the audience got to vote on how they thought the story should turn out."

"Maybe if we sing and dance," Sam said with a smile, "it will help us figure out the right ending."

Mr. Pruitt stood up and put on his coat. No longer Elvis Presley, he now looked like the mild-mannered teacher of sixth-grade English that he normally was. He threw a scarf around his neck and said, "Well, let me know when you have *The Mystery of Edwin Drood* all figured out."

Joe glanced at his watch, noticing it was a little after three o'clock. David had now been officially missing for over three hours. As Joe stared at his watch, he felt more and more tense with each movement of the second hand.

"Right now," Joe said quietly, "I think I'm more concerned with figuring out The Mystery of David Barnes."

Chapter Nine

Joe noticed a line of black clouds sailing through the sky, signaling that a storm might be on its way. The search team of Joe, Sam, and Wishbone was headed back to the Talbot house. Joe figured that he and Sam could grab a quick bite to eat, then call some of David's other friends. It was possible one of them would have some idea about David's whereabouts.

Suddenly, a dark thought entered Joe's mind. He broke into a run and called out, "Sam, follow me!"

"What is it?" Sam said, as she and Wishbone caught up to Joe.

"I just realized something," Joe explained. "We know that David left Mr. Pruitt's house around eleven this morning. That means he might have gone home around eleven-fifteen. He was supposed to meet with us at noon. Let's say he decided to use that spare time fiddling with something in his garage."

"But we knocked on the garage door earlier," Sam said. "We know he wasn't there."

"We know he didn't *answer*," Joe pointed out. "There's a difference."

"I'm sure David wouldn't ignore us."

"David works with electricity a lot. More than a few

80

times, he's blown fuses and even given himself some mild electrical shocks."

A worried look crossed Sam's face. "What are you saying? That David might have electrocuted himself? That maybe he was in the garage, but he was too injured to answer us?"

"I'm not saying that's what happened, Sam, but it's possible."

Joe, Sam, and Wishbone continued to run. After winding their way through a few short blocks, they reached the garage of the Barnes's house.

Joe banged on the garage door, shouting, "David, are you in there? It's Joe! David, are you there?"

Joe tried to lift the door, but it was locked.

There was no reply. But, of course, that was the point. Joe knew that if David were seriously injured, or even unconscious, he wouldn't be able to answer. Joe remembered that the Barneses had a window on the side of the garage. "Sam, let's look through the side window."

When they reached the window, Joe peered inside and gave a quick look around. Then he released a big sigh of relief. David was definitely not in there.

"Good, he's not here," Joe said.

Sam looked relieved also. "Oh, let's see if we can spot anything that might be helpful to us. You know, see if there's some sort of clue."

Joe's eyes looked around the garage. Enough light streamed in through the window so that Joe could see well. Various pieces of equipment and tools lay scattered on David's worktable. It looked as if David had recently been building something, but Joe had no idea what that might be. David was always in the middle of assembling or inventing some unusual item.

Joe spotted a piece of paper lying on the work-table. He could see that a few words had been written in David's neat handwriting. As Joe squinted, the words gradually came into focus. They read: "Set for AU."

"I see a bunch of mechanical stuff," Joe said. "Do you see that note?" Joe asked Sam, pointing to the worktable. "It says 'Set for AU.'"

"Yes, I see it," Sam said.

"Do you see anything else in there that could give us a clue?" asked Joe.

"Not really."

Joe turned to Sam. "Well, the good news is that David's not lying helpless on the garage floor. The bad news is that we still don't know where he is. I wonder if that note is any kind of clue."

"'Set for AU,'" Sam said slowly. "What could that possibly mean?"

Joe and Sam stood there by the window for a few moments, thinking. Wishbone stood beside them. He, too, seemed to be deep in thought.

Joe tapped Sam on the shoulder. "I've got an idea.

Maybe the note was a reminder for David to get a Christmas present for Alan Underwood."

"Alan Underwood?" Sam said, looking puzzled. "That real big kid who's in the seventh grade? David barely knows him. I don't see why he would be getting Alan Underwood a present. Besides, the note said 'set,' not 'get.'"

"True," Joe admitted.

Sam tapped Joe on the shoulder. "Instead of 'AU,' could it have been 'AV'? I think that's some type of electrical current."

"No, I'm certain it was 'AU.' Anyway, the current you're referring to is 'AC.'"

"Oh, that's right."

In his mind, Joe stared at the note, all the while thinking, *Set for AU . . . Set for AU . . . Set for AU. . . .*

Not a single idea was coming to Joe. He stomped his foot in frustration and said, "Where *is* he?!"

"Take it easy," Sam said. "Why don't we go over to your house and make those phone calls? Maybe one of David's other friends will know what's going on."

Joe ran to the front porch of the Barnes house and rang the bell, just in case someone had come home. There was no answer. As Joe and Sam walked toward the Talbot house, Joe called to Wishbone, "Are you coming, boy?"

"If it's okay with the two of you," Wishbone replied, "I'll wait for you out here. I've got some . . . uh . . . business to take care of."

As soon as Joe and Sam went inside the Talbot house, Wishbone darted into Wanda's yard. He stopped when he came to the fountain with the yellow elephant on it. He decided he would do some more searching for the rawhide bone, just in case he had overlooked it earlier. However, after examining the area carefully with both his eyes and nose, the dog found no sign of the bone.

Doggone it! Wishbone thought as he left the backyard. *Someone* must *have stolen that bone. But who would do such a thing?*

As Wishbone entered Wanda's front yard, he saw Wanda's white convertible pull up in the driveway. After climbing out of her car, Wanda pointed a finger at Wishbone. In a stern tone of voice, she said, "I didn't say anything a little while ago in front of Joe and Sam. But I saw what you and your friends did to my garden this morning. And I am not pleased!"

"Huh?" Wishbone said, tilting his head. "What are you talking about?"

Wishbone had an ongoing battle with Wanda. Wanda believed her yard was to be used mostly for the planting and growing of flowers. Wishbone believed the yard was to be used mostly for bone burial and other forms of dog business and entertainment. Much of the time, Wishbone and Wanda were able to share the yard in peace. And yet, other times . . . there were misunderstandings.

"You have been misbehaving, Wishbone!" Wanda scolded. Then she opened the trunk of her car and began to pull out bags of groceries.

Could Wanda have possibly taken the bone? Wishbone wondered.

Wishbone thought back to that all-important time, shortly before the hour of noon. While he and Sparkey were chasing the gray cat, Wanda had leaned out her window and yelled some words. Suddenly, Wishbone remembered that Wanda's words had something to do with not bothering her garden. Wishbone also seemed to remember a flower bulb flying up in the air. Maybe that was what Wanda was referring to when she spoke about Wishbone messing up her garden. After the cat had raced up the tree, Wishbone had gone to give Joe a greeting.

Then he had run back to the garden to retrieve the bone. But the bone was gone.

As Wanda carried some grocery bags into her house, Wishbone realized that Wanda could have taken the bone while he was off greeting Joe.

Wanda isn't a mean person, Wishbone thought. *But she seemed really upset just now. Maybe she took the bone as a way of teaching me a lesson.*

Wanda came outside again. She shot Wishbone an impatient look. Then she began to pull more bags from the car.

Bingo! I'll bet myself anything that she did it. I need solid proof, though. Even humans are innocent until proven guilty. If I can somehow get a sniff of Wanda's paws . . . I mean hands, I'll know right away whether she came into contact with that bone.

Wishbone nudged Wanda's leg with his muzzle. "Hey, Wanda, I'm sorry about that silly business with the garden. How about giving me a neighborly pat?"

Wanda gave the dog an annoyed glance. Then she set her bags on the ground.

This isn't going to be so easy. Wanda's not in a great mood. Besides, she's not a big petter in the first place. All right, time to dig into my bag of cute dog tricks.

Wishbone ran into the middle of Wanda's yard, let loose a yip, then lay on his side. He rolled his way across the ground, turning his body over and over. "Look at me, Wanda! I'm rolling around in the grass!"

Wanda shut the trunk of the car, not even noticing the dog.

Wishbone got up and called, "Hey! Watch this! I can do such a cool jump!"

Wishbone ran a short distance. Then he leaped straight up in the air, as if catching a stick.

Wanda gathered two bags in her arms and headed for her front door. She didn't seem to be enjoying the show.

Wishbone ran straight into Wanda's path, blocking her way. He lay on his belly, flopped down his ears, and placed a paw softly on his muzzle, as if to say, "I'm a shy, cute little dog, aren't I?"

Wanda looked at Wishbone, her expression softening. In a childlike tone, she said, "Oh, I guess you are an awfully cute fella."

With a hidden smile, Wishbone thought, *Those tricks may be a bit sneaky, but they work every time!*

Wanda set down her bags again and leaned over to give Wishbone a friendly scratch on the neck. Wishbone craned his head around to catch a good sniff of Wanda's hand. There was not the slightest trace of rawhide bone with beef flavoring. He moved to Wanda's other side, forcing her to scratch his neck with her other hand. There was no trace of beef or bone there, either.

"Thanks," Wishbone told Wanda. "I see you're not the bone burglar, after all. Sorry I had to make you go through with that examination, but it was necessary."

Wanda picked up her grocery bags and walked away. The moment she stepped inside her house, Joe and Sam stepped out of the Talbot house. Wishbone ran over to join them.

"Well, we didn't learn anything about David," Sam told Joe. "But thanks for the sandwich. We missed lunch and I sure was hungry."

"Sandwich?" Wishbone said, aiming an accusing look at Joe. "Why wasn't I invited? I've told you over and over—"

"It's three-thirty," Sam said, glancing at her watch. "I've got to be at Pepper Pete's at four. I'm sorry to leave you, Joe, but my dad's counting on me to help serve. Let me know the second you find out anything about David."

Joe nodded. Wishbone knew that Sam's father owned Pepper Pete's Pizza Parlor, in downtown Oakdale. Sam worked there several nights a week.

As Sam walked away, Wishbone turned to Joe. "What's

next, big guy? Looks like it's up to you and me now to find David."

"Three-thirty," Joe said to himself, worry written all over his face. "I don't like this at all. I guess I'll just start walking. Hopefully, I'll either see David or get a brilliant idea of where he might be."

With a determined look, Joe signaled for Wishbone to follow. The boy and dog walked to a wooded area behind David's house. There, they picked up the trail of a narrow stream.

Where the Dickens is David? Wishbone thought, as he watched the stream trickle over the rocks. *I sure hope nothing bad has happened to him. David's one of the greatest guys I know. He's a wonderful son, brother, friend, scientist, mechanic, and back scratcher. We've just gotta find him!*

As more black clouds gathered in the sky, the air turned colder. Wishbone's nose picked up a heavy, damp smell that told him a storm was very near. Storms were not Wishbone's favorite thing. He disliked the way all of a sudden several million gallons of water came pouring out of the sky, often joined by some very loud thunder.

Soon the stream led Joe and Wishbone into the tree-filled land of Jackson Park. Normally, Wishbone loved the park, but right now it seemed threatening. A shadowy gloom hung over the wintry landscape, and no one was around, animal or man. Gusts of cold, biting wind blew by, shaking the bare branches into a chorus of eerie rattling.

It seems like that mysterious wind from last night is coming back, Wishbone thought with concern. *As if it hasn't caused enough problems already.*

Wishbone saw the gray limbs of an oak tree waving wildly at him. It seemed as if the tree was warning him to run from this place.

Wishbone's tail flicked with alarm. He saw someone or something leap out from behind the trunk of the tree!

Chapter Ten

"Boo!" a voice yelled as a figure leaped out from behind the tree trunk.

Joe jumped back, startled. He noticed that Wishbone did the same. After recovering from the shock, Joe realized it was only someone trying to scare him. And he was surprised to see that the someone was Lola Hernandez.

Wishbone gave a growl.

"Why did you do that?" Joe asked Lola, a bit upset by her prank.

Lola glared at Joe. Her black hair was being tossed around by the steady wind. "Because I felt like it."

Joe could see that Lola was still angry, the way she had been at the antiques store. He figured that was why Lola had tried to scare him. But he still had no idea why she was angry. Joe decided to bring up the subject.

"Lola, I get the feeling that you're angry with me for some reason."

"Maybe I am. Maybe I'm not."

"Okay." Joe didn't know how to respond to that. Finally, he said, "What are you doing around here?"

"For your information, I'm looking for my brother, Luis. He left the house early this morning, and I haven't seen him since. Have you seen him, by any chance?"

Joe rubbed his chin. "No, I haven't. But people seem to be disappearing left and right today."

"What do you mean?"

"You know how Sam, Chloe, David, and I were supposed to get together today to work on a school assignment? Well, David never showed up, so we ended the meeting early. For the past few hours, Sam and I have been looking all over Oakdale for David."

Lola seemed surprised by this news. "Is that what you were doing when I saw you in that antiques store?"

"That's right."

A smile came across Lola's lips. Joe could see she was suddenly back to her friendly self.

"Well, I'm sure David is all right," Lola assured Joe.

"And I'm sure Luis is all right, too," Joe said. He was puzzled, though, by Lola's quick change in attitude.

"I know. I just worry about him."

"Because he likes to do dangerous things?" Joe asked.

Lola leaned against the tree she had hidden behind and began to twist a finger, as if she were suddenly upset about something. "That's part of it."

"What's the rest of it?"

"Oh, it's nothing."

"Come on, tell me."

Lola looked at Joe, as if deciding whether she could trust him. "I probably shouldn't tell you this, but . . . Luis has had some problems in the past."

"What kind of problems?" Joe asked, growing interested. He noticed that Wishbone's ears were on full alert.

"He used to get into all kinds of trouble," Lola said, still twisting her finger. "He did some small shoplifting, and . . . uh . . . well, he also got into a couple of fights—you know, with other boys his age. He promised me that he's finished with those kinds of things. He's stayed clear of any kind of trouble for a while now. So I'm sure he's just fine, but . . . that's why I worry."

Joe remembered Luis's moody behavior from the night before. It fit together with what Joe was now hearing about the boy.

"I'm sorry to hear that Luis was having these problems," Joe said. "I'll keep a lookout for him. And maybe you'll keep a lookout for David. With both of us wandering around, we're bound to run into at least one of them."

"Hopefully . . ." Lola said, giving Joe a friendly punch on the arm. Then Lola walked away. Soon she disappeared behind a curtain of trees.

Joe and Wishbone walked in the opposite direction, still following the course of the stream. *It's ten past four,* Joe realized as he checked his watch. *Where is David? Where is David? I need to find him. This is so weird!*

Joe looked down to watch the stream flowing steadily over the rocks. He was reminded of a chapter in *The Mystery of Edwin Drood.* The night after the storm in Cloisterham, a minister strolling along a river noticed something shining in the water. He dove in and discovered that the shining object was a watch engraved with the initials "E.D." The watch had belonged to Edwin Drood. But there was no sign of Edwin—dead or alive—anywhere in the area.

Joe felt a sudden shiver go up his spine. He wondered if something like that could have happened to David, his neighbor. Joe had never thought about the possibility of David suddenly not being around. David was one of those parts of Joe's life that was always there. Whenever Joe wanted company or had a math question or wished to seek out a new adventure, he just walked next door and gave a knock. Simple as that. He had never spent any time thinking about how wonderful this was—until now.

Joe found himself wondering if Luis might have done something to David. Luis had a history of getting into fights. Besides, he did think David had insulted him the night before. Joe wondered if Luis might have accidentally met up with David, or even purposely looked for him, and then . . . Joe didn't want to think about that possibility.

Joe sat on a large rock by the stream. Wishbone sat quietly beside him. Joe pulled *The Mystery of Edwin Drood* from his backpack and looked at the gold-colored lettering stamped on the cover. When he opened the book, a gust of wind blew by, flipping the pages.

The pages stopped flipping at a page with an illustration of Neville Landless. Neville was holding up a fist in anger. He had the same dark Gypsy-like features and fierce eyes as his sister, Helena. A caption showed what Neville was saying: "The plain truth is, I am still angry when I recall that night."

Staring at the picture, Joe thought about the book's plot. If someone *had* murdered Edwin Drood, John Jasper was the most likely suspect. It seemed that Jasper had

gotten Neville to quarrel with Edwin, so Neville would seem guilty once Jasper had done away with Edwin. Then, again, Neville had quarreled bitterly with Edwin, and he could have actually been the murderer.

Joe realized that qualities about Neville and Luis were mixing together in his mind. Joe didn't like the idea that Luis might have gotten hold of David. But that ugly idea was growing stronger by the second.

"I need to find Luis," Joe told himself as he returned the book to his backpack. "I need to find Luis as soon as possible. I need to find out if he knows anything about David's disappearance. Right now, it's the only lead I have. So . . . where could Luis have gone?"

Wishbone's eyes were attracted to the water tower. Beyond a stretch of trees, the metal tower stood against the black clouds like a fairy-tale giant.

"Maybe Luis is up on the water tower," Wishbone told Joe.

Joe looked at the dog, not seeming to understand.

"Remember last night?" Wishbone said, rising to his feet. "Luis said he was interested in climbing the town water tower. In fact, that's what caused the problem between Luis and David. David said climbing the tower would be a stupid thing to do. Luis thought David was calling him stupid . . . or something like that."

Joe didn't say anything. Wishbone pointed his muzzle at the water tower and gave a sharp bark.

Joe looked in the direction Wishbone was trying to point out to him. "Hey! The water tower," he said softly. "Maybe *that's* where Luis is. Come on, Wishbone."

"I thought you'd never ask," Wishbone said, as he and Joe headed for the water tower.

After making their way through the park, Joe and Wishbone came to the clearing where the water tower stood. Several very long metal legs rose upward to support a huge, rounded water tank.

Wishbone tilted back his head to examine the top of the tower. A narrow platform with a railing ran all the way around the water tank. Wishbone saw the shape of a person standing on the platform. Focusing his eyes sharply, Wishbone noticed that the person was wearing a black jacket—very much like the leather jacket Luis wore the night before.

Joe seemed to notice the same thing. He cupped his hands to his mouth and called up. "Hey! Luis, is that you up there?"

The figure on the tower leaned over the railing and looked down. He stared in the direction of Joe and Wishbone but didn't say anything. Wishbone was now certain it was Luis.

Joe called, "It's me—Joe Talbot!"

Luis remained silent. Even though Luis was a great distance away, Wishbone could sense anger coming from the boy.

I'm getting a bad feeling about this kid, Wishbone thought tensely. *As in very bad.*

"Why don't you come down from there?" Joe called. "I want to talk with you!"

Luis's voice drifted down from the top of the tower. "Why don't *you* come up?"

It sounded more like a threat than an invitation.

Joe glanced at a ladder that ran up the side of the tower. Wishbone knew his buddy was weighing the danger of climbing the tower against his desire to see if Luis knew anything about David. Joe looked down at Wishbone, as if seeking advice.

"It's a risky business," Wishbone told Joe. "On the one paw, that's a long climb. Besides, Luis may not be too nice when you finally get up there. On the other paw, we've got to find out what happened to David. It's your choice, pal."

"Wait right here for me," Joe told Wishbone.

Joe walked over to the ladder. He set down his backpack. Then he placed his foot on the lowest rung. . . .

Chapter Eleven

One step after another, Joe made his way slowly and very carefully up the steep rungs of the ladder. Up and up and up . . .

The higher Joe climbed, the stronger the wind seemed to blow. His hair was whipped back and forth, and the wind's force actually rocked his body.

Keeping a firm grip on the ladder, Joe glanced up to see Luis staring over the railing at him. The boy's black hair and jacket created a threatening sight. Though Joe couldn't see the face very well, he felt as if Luis's eyes were burning a hole in him.

If Luis likes to get into fights, and he's angry at me to begin with, Joe thought, *it could be awfully dangerous up there. What if we get into a scuffle? What if I—*

Joe paused, having second thoughts about continuing his climb. He quickly glanced down to see if he was closer to the bottom or top of the ladder. Far below, he saw the tops of the gray, swaying trees. Then, even farther below, he saw a white blur with dark spots, which he realized was Wishbone.

A wave of dizziness swept over Joe. His head felt as light as a feather, and his legs seemed as if they weren't even there. Joe's mind was overcome with thoughts of falling through space, racing head over heels for the distant ground.

A blast of wind blew Joe sideways. One foot slipped from the ladder and was left dangling. For a heart-stopping second, Joe thought he was a goner.

But Joe realized he still had a firm grip with both hands and one foot. Joe returned his eyes to the ladder and took a deep breath.

I made it this far up, so I can make it the rest of the way. For David's sake. I have to find out what happened to him, and Luis might know. . . . Okay, don't think about anything but the ladder. You can do this, Joe.

Rung after rung, step after careful step, Joe made his way upward. He knew he was now rising extremely high off the ground, but he didn't let his mind dwell on that fact. The wind seemed to roar straight through his ears, and the rungs looked as if they were never-ending, but Joe kept climbing. After what seemed like forever, Joe finally stepped onto the metal platform that ran around the top of the water tank.

Even though his feet finally rested on a solid surface, Joe didn't relax. The tingling that ran through his body told him not to let down his guard for a single second.

Joe saw the tall figure of Luis walking toward him. Unlike Joe, Luis seemed completely comfortable at this dizzying height. Luis stopped a few feet away.

"Hi," Joe said, wrapping a hand around the railing. "What are you doing up here?"

"Just hanging out," Luis said, a challenging glare in his eyes.

"Do you know where my friend David is?"

"No, I don't."

Joe didn't want to make Luis any angrier than he seemed to be already. Still, he hadn't climbed all this way only to give up easily.

"Are you sure that you don't know where he is?" Joe asked.

Luis's eyes narrowed. "Yes, I'm sure. Now, why don't you leave me alone?"

Joe studied Luis's face. He searched for a sign that the boy might be hiding some dark deed.

"Your sister's been looking for you," Joe mentioned.

"So . . ."

"She's afraid you might . . . uh . . . be getting into some kind of trouble."

"Well, I'm not!" Luis snapped with rage.

Joe clutched the railing even more tightly. The knuckles on his hand turned white. He asked, "What have you been doing today?"

"Stuff . . ."

"Like what?"

Luis took a threatening step forward.

Joe felt his heart pounding a mile a minute. He thought, *I've never been in a serious fight, and I sure don't want to start now. Especially not with someone who has a history of being in fights. And especially not at this height!*

"What do you care what I've been doing?" Luis said in a snarling voice. "It seems that I'm not good enough for you and your friends to hang out with!"

Joe tried very hard not to show the nervousness he was feeling. "Why do you say that?"

Luis closed the distance between himself and Joe. He stuck a finger right in Joe's face, as if he were itching to get a fight going. "Last night, Lola and I talked about getting together with you and your friends. You said today was no good because you would be busy with some school assignment. But it doesn't look to me like you're busy with any school assignment. It looks to me like you're just wandering around with your dog. It's pretty clear that you and your friends were just trying to think of a way to get rid of us!"

At once, everything made some sense to Joe. When Lola saw Joe and Sam in the antiques store, she thought they had been lying when they said they would be busy today. Now Luis thought the same thing. Lola and Luis believed that Joe, Sam, and David had lied to avoid spending time with them. No wonder they both seemed angry. Joe remembered that Lola seemed less angry after Joe had told her about David not showing up for the *Edwin Drood* discussion.

"Look," Joe said, "you've got it all wrong, Luis. We *were* planning to work on that assignment today. But then David never showed up. Sam and I got worried about him. We've spent most of the day looking for him all over town. That's what I'm doing right now. I thought you might know something about where he was."

For a tense moment, Joe heard only the whooshing of wind.

"Is that the truth?" Luis asked suspiciously.

"That's the honest truth," Joe assured Luis.

Luis turned away from Joe and leaned on the railing. The anger seemed to be draining out of him, like air seeping out of a balloon.

Finally, he said, "Oh, I'm sorry I accused you like that. I guess . . . I get really bent out of shape by that kind of thing—being brushed off, I mean."

"Why do you get so bent out of shape by that?" Joe said, going to lean on the railing next to Luis.

"Ah, forget it."

"No, I'd really like to know."

Luis ran a hand through his black hair, obviously uncomfortable with the subject. "Well, because of my dad's job, every few years Lola and I have to move to a new place. And . . . uh . . . with all that wandering, it's tough making friends."

"But I thought you liked living all over the country. It sounds pretty cool to me."

Luis gave a snort. "It's not as cool as you might think it is."

"It's not?"

"This guy, David. How long have you and him been friends?"

"All of our lives."

"I hate to sound like a crybaby," Luis said, meeting Joe's eyes, "but I don't have any friends like that. By the time I start getting to be buddies with somebody, it's time for my family to move somewhere else. And it's not so easy making those friends in the first place. People already have their own crowd. They're not really looking for anybody new. After a while, I just gave up trying to make good friends at all. The whole thing was such a hassle."

"I see what you mean," Joe said sympathetically.

Luis seemed embarrassed by the conversation, but he continued anyway. "I guess that's why I do all that dangerous stuff. Like climbing this tower. I guess . . . I'm just looking for something to entertain myself. For a while I was even . . . Oh, forget it. You don't need to hear my whole life story."

Joe realized Luis had been at the point of mentioning the fighting and shoplifting. He also realized that he liked Luis. He regretted that the boy would be in Oakdale for only a few weeks.

Joe tapped the arm of Luis's jacket. "Well, my friends and I weren't giving you and Lola the cold shoulder. In fact, we can do things together while you're in town. Sam will hang out with us, too. So will David—if I can find him, that is."

"I'd like that," Luis said with a sudden, warm smile. "We don't even have to do anything this dangerous. You have to admit, though, that it's a really cool view from way up here."

Joe agreed and they both sat down. Relaxed, Joe looked around. He realized he wasn't nearly as nervous

about the height as he had been a few moments ago. Darkness came very early this time of year, and dusk was already beginning to dim the sky.

Through the fading light, Joe saw the entire town of Oakdale spread before him. There was the park, the downtown area, the many blocks with all the many houses, the drive-in movie theater, the railroad tracks. The scene looked a lot like a toy village from a giant-sized train set.

Then Joe realized there was still one item he couldn't see—David.

"We'd better get down from here," Joe told Luis. "You need to go find your sister so she can stop worrying about you. And I need to find David."

"I guess you're right," Luis said, getting up and moving away from the railing. "I'll let you go first."

Joe stood up and headed for the ladder, then carefully lowered his foot onto the top rung.

"Remember," Luis cautioned Joe, "you'll be okay if you don't look down."

"Don't look down!" Wishbone called up to Joe.

Wishbone watched as both Joe and Luis began to climb down the tower's ladder. The dog was very curious to know what had happened up on the platform. Meanwhile, he could see that Joe was okay.

Wishbone lay down, figuring it would take Joe a few minutes to make it to the ground. The air was turning colder by the minute. The dog rubbed his belly into the grass for warmth. Through the dim light, Wishbone saw a creature skittering by, graceful as a ballet dancer. He realized it was the very same cat he and Sparkey had chased that morning.

Hey! Could the gray cat have made off with the bone? Wishbone wondered.

Wishbone thought back to that important moment, shortly before noontime. While he and Sparkey had been arguing over the bone, the cat had come by. Wishbone and Sparkey had chased the cat around for a while. The cat hadn't seemed too pleased by that. After the cat had hightailed it up the tree, Wishbone had gone to greet Joe. Then he had run back to Wanda's yard to retrieve the bone. But the bone was gone.

As the gray cat continued to skitter by, Wishbone realized that the cat could have taken the bone while he was off greeting Joe.

Cats don't usually go for bones, Wishbone reasoned. *But the cat might have been so annoyed about being chased that she made off with the bone just to get even.*

Wishbone watched the cat stop to lick a paw.

Ha! I bet she's trying to clean off the evidence right now.

But all the perfumes of France won't hide that beef flavor. Still, I need solid proof. I suppose even cats are innocent until proven guilty. I need just one good sniff of that sneaky feline's paws. Then I'll know for sure if she's a cat burglar or not.

But there was a problem. Wishbone could not remember the last time he had gotten within two feet of a cat. Whenever he approached a cat, even if he wasn't planning on a chase, the cat went racing away.

As quietly as possible, Wishbone got up on all fours. He lowered his body, bent back his ears, and crept ever so slowly in the cat's direction. He was hoping to catch the cat by surprise, before she had a chance to flee up the nearest tree.

The dog's tracking skills were A-1, and he got halfway there. But then, stopping in mid-lick, the cat suddenly turned and spotted Wishbone. She was up and racing away without so much as a friendly hello.

Wishbone darted after the cat for all he was worth. He gained on her, getting closer and closer. When the cat began to turn toward a tree, Wishbone knew he had only seconds left.

Don't climb up the tree, don't climb up the tree, don't climb up the—

Fast as a flash, the cat scampered up the side of the tree. Wishbone skidded to a stop, panting hard. That was the way almost every single cat chase he had ever been in had ended.

Wishbone looked up and saw the cat standing on a branch. The cat stared down at him with her green eyes, as if to say, "Too bad dogs can't climb, isn't it?"

If she's watching me, maybe I can figure out a way to get her down here. The "cute" trick won't work, I'm pretty sure of that. But there's got to be . . .

Wishbone knew that sometimes one dog would lie on his back to show that he was weaker than another dog. That was usually done to avoid a fight. Being a brave and fearless dog, Wishbone had never used that method himself. But he was familiar with it, and he figured that maybe the cat would be, too.

Wishbone lay down on his back, his belly in the air. For good measure, he tried to put a look of helplessness on his face.

Oh, boy, it's killing me to have to do this. I'd better at least get some good results.

Wishbone could see that the cat was watching him closely. She was trying to figure out what was going on. She seemed to be falling for Wishbone's act. Sure enough, the cat walked along the branch, then scampered down the trunk of the tree to the ground.

As Wishbone remained on his back, the cat came toward the dog, ever so cautiously. She began to circle Wishbone, trying to figure out what was on the "cowardly" dog's mind. Finally, the cat walked right up to Wishbone and reached out a paw to touch his belly.

Wishbone lifted his head and grabbed a good sniff of the cat's front paws. The cat backed away very quickly, but Wishbone had gotten what he needed. He detected absolutely no scent of rawhide bone with beef flavoring. That was too bad, because it meant Wishbone was fresh out of ideas about how and where the bone had disappeared.

Wishbone rolled over and came to a standing position. "Okay, kitty, you're off the hook. Thanks for your cooperation. You can be on your way now."

The cat didn't leave, though. Instead she focused her glowing green eyes on Wishbone. The dog didn't have a clue about what the cat was thinking. Wishbone felt a bit confused. He had never been this close to a cat before, and he had no idea what was expected of him. For a few long moments, the dog and the cat just stared at each other without making a sound.

Uh . . . this is getting a little embarrassing. I wish someone would help me out here.

A jagged bolt of lightning suddenly shot through the darkening sky.

Wishbone felt his whiskers twitching, and the cat scampered away in fright.

Chapter Twelve

Joe heard a rumble of distant thunder as he and Wishbone walked at a quick pace. Darkness had fallen. The air was filled with the threat of the coming storm. After saying good-bye to Luis, Joe had decided he would pass through the downtown area once more. If he still saw no sign of David, perhaps he would head home.

When Joe arrived downtown, the white holiday lights along Oak Street glowed cheerily against the darkness. A few people were hurrying to their cars to beat the storm, but the area was mostly deserted. A sheet of newspaper flew down the street, as if being chased by the wind.

The clock on top of the town hall building sounded five loud clangs, signaling it was now five o'clock.

David's been missing for five hours, Joe thought, feeling each clang deep in his head.

Joe spotted Dan Bloodgood wheeling his cart toward the post office. "Hi, Mr. Bloodgood," Joe called, as he and Wishbone ran over to him. "Have you seen David yet?"

Mr. Bloodgood stopped his cart. "No, I haven't, Joe. Sorry. You look awfully worried about something, son."

"I am," Joe admitted.

"Sit down with me a minute," the mail carrier said. "Tell me what's going on."

Joe liked Mr. Bloodgood. Though he wasn't very old, the man had a wise way about him. Joe sat on the bench in front of the post office and put Wishbone on his lap. Mr. Bloodgood sat beside them. Then Joe gave Mr. Bloodgood a review of the day's events.

"And you have no other ideas about where David could be?" Mr. Bloodgood asked when Joe was finished.

"No, I don't," Joe answered.

"Maybe you need to clear your mind," Mr. Bloodgood suggested. "Sometimes if you're concentrating too hard on one single thing, your thoughts get all mixed up and confused. Let's talk about something else for a few minutes. Have you done anything interesting during your winter break?"

Joe told Mr. Bloodgood about the *Edwin Drood* assignment.

"Is that a good book, *The Mystery of Edwin Drood?*" Mr. Bloodgood asked.

"It's great. You actually remind me of one of the characters in it."

"Me? Why?"

"His name is Durdles, and he's this stonemason who spends a lot of time in the town's burial tomb."

"In the burial tomb?" Mr. Bloodgood said with surprise. "Isn't that the underground area where they used to bury dead bodies?"

"That's right."

"Why do I remind you of this fellow?"

"Because Durdles is always wandering around the town. Everyone seems to know and like him—just like the way people in Oakdale feel about you. He also keeps a bunch of keys in his pockets that are always rattling around. And you keep lots of keys on your key chain, too."

"I see," Mr. Bloodgood said with a smile.

Joe heard a thudding sound. He turned to see a cardboard box blowing down the street. The wind was really kicking up, the way it had the previous night.

"One night," Joe told the mail carrier, "this character named John Jasper goes with Durdles down into the burial chamber. It's a creepy scene. There's dust and cobwebs everywhere. While he's down there, Jasper steals a key to one of the tombs, and he learns from Durdles about quicklime. That's a type of powder that can dissolve a human body, or most anything—except for metal."

"Sounds to me like this Jasper character is up to no good," Mr. Bloodgood remarked.

"The book gives you the impression that he was thinking of murdering his nephew, Edwin Drood. And you also get the idea that he was thinking of stashing the body in the tomb that he stole the key for. And then it seems that he plans to dissolve the body with quicklime. But you never find out if that's what Jasper really did."

Mr. Bloodgood chuckled. "Is this the kind of stuff they're teaching you kids in school?"

"I guess it sounds pretty gory for an eighth-grade school assignment," Joe said with a grin. As quick as the grin came, it faded. "But I've been thinking about the book a lot lately. It's almost been haunting me like a ghost. Maybe that's because it's a mystery that can never be solved."

"That does make it interesting. Frustrating too, I suspect."

Joe rubbed Wishbone's back, hoping to warm both himself and the dog. "To tell you the truth, I've come across a bunch of mysteries lately that I just can't seem to solve—like, what happened to Edwin Drood, what happened to David Barnes, and what happened to my dad's ring. I didn't tell you about that yet. A few days ago, I lost this gold class ring that had belonged to my father."

"Oh, I'm sorry to hear that. I know how much you value your father's things."

Joe glanced up at the dark sky. Though he didn't mention it, that was another mystery he had never been able to figure out—why his father had to die so early in life.

Mr. Bloodgood put a hand on Joe's shoulder. "Not all mysteries are meant to be solved. Some are, but . . . well, some aren't. Native Americans, such as myself, believe that your father's spirit will always be living somewhere inside of your own spirit."

"I know," Joe said quietly.

After a moment, Mr. Bloodgood said, "Well, now that you've given your mind a rest, do you have any fresh ideas about where David might be?"

Joe's mind actually did feel a little more clear. "You know, he could be home by now. I haven't checked in at the Barnes house for over an hour."

"Why don't you head over there and see?" Mr. Bloodgood said as he stood. "You need to be getting home, anyway. That storm's right over us, and I don't want you to get caught in it. I'm done with my rounds, but I'll take the long route home and keep an eye out for David."

Joe set Wishbone on the ground and rose to his feet. "Thanks for talking to me, Mr. Bloodgood."

"That's what I'm here for," Mr. Bloodgood said with a friendly wave. "That, and delivering the mail."

"And delivering dog treats," Wishbone pointed out.

As Mr. Bloodgood went inside the post office to drop off his mail cart, Wishbone and Joe continued on their way. They left the glowing lights of downtown. Next, they came to the dark stretch south of town that led to the Talbots' neighborhood. They passed by the empty grounds of Sequoyah Middle School. Thunder grumbled several times, reminding Wishbone of a Doberman's menacing growls.

Wishbone turned his head, seeing a shape hurrying along the railroad tracks, just beyond the school. Then . . . Wishbone thought he caught a whiff of David in the air.

Wishbone dashed over to the object to find that it was a baseball cap blowing in the wind. Holding down the cap with a paw, he saw the symbol of a computer company. After a good, deep sniff, the dog knew for sure that the cap belonged to David.

Wishbone grabbed the cap in his mouth and ran back to Joe. The boy started to take the cap from Wishbone and said, "Look, we don't have time . . . Wait! This is David's cap!"

Wishbone knew that the cap might have just blown off David's head, and that alone didn't mean anything. Even so, finding the cap gave the dog a bad feeling. Wishbone sensed that Joe felt the same way.

"Follow me!" Joe called as he ran toward the nearby

train station. Once there, Joe went to a pay phone that was underneath the roof of the waiting platform. He put a quarter into the slot and dialed a number. Wishbone raised his ears. His hearing was so sharp that he could usually make out both ends of a phone conversation.

"Hello," a voice said into the phone. Wishbone recognized the voice of David's mother.

"Hello, Mrs. Barnes. This is Joe. Is David there?"

"No, he isn't," Mrs. Barnes replied. "Mr. Barnes, Emily, and I were gone for the day. But this morning David told me he would be home by five at the latest. Do you have any idea where he is?"

"Uh . . . no, I don't."

Joe was trying to sound calm. Wishbone knew that was because he didn't want to get Mrs. Barnes upset.

"I'm beginning to get worried," Mrs. Barnes said. "David always calls if he's busy with something away from the house. He's very responsible that way. But it's twenty past five now, and I haven't heard a word from him. There's no message on the phone machine, either. Are you sure you don't know where he might be?"

"No, I really don't."

Thunder boomed, loud as a cannon shot.

"I wonder if I should call the police," Mrs. Barnes said with a slight tremble in her voice.

"Look, I'm sure he's okay," Joe said calmly. "Like you said, David is very responsible. But . . . well, maybe you should give the police a call anyway. In the meantime, I'll look for him and I'll let you know the second I find anything. But I'm really sure everything is okay."

"Thank you, Joe."

Joe hung up the phone, seeming very concerned.

Wishbone sensed something else blowing in the mysterious wind—danger.

Chapter Thirteen

Finally, the storm hit full force.

Sheets of rain poured down from the sky, hammering at the wooden roof of the train's waiting platform. Joe watched the rain slice through the darkness, slashing at the ground. He noticed Wishbone watching the downpour with a nervous expression.

I've got to find David, Joe thought desperately. *No matter what! This is one mystery that is not going to be unsolved!*

Joe sat on a bench and stared at the baseball cap. Ignoring the weather's wetness and chill, he tried to focus his thoughts. Joe wanted to think only about David.

Instead, however, he found himself pulled back, almost against his will, to *The Mystery of Edwin Drood.* Finding David's baseball cap reminded Joe of how Edwin Drood's watch had been found in the river. Joe began to wonder why only the watch had been discovered in the river. If someone had killed Edwin, then tossed his body into the river, where was the body?

Suddenly, Joe realized something important. As Joe had told Mr. Bloodgood, John Jasper might have been planning to dissolve Edwin's body with quicklime so that it could never be identified. Maybe Jasper really *had* carried out this plan. Then, afterward, he threw Edwin's watch into the river, knowing that the quicklime would not dissolve the watch because it was made of metal.

Then Joe realized something else. Jasper did not know that Edwin was carrying an engagement ring in his coat pocket. He had planned to give the ring to Rosa Bud. He had held off from doing so, because he was not certain he really wanted to marry her. The ring, however, probably stayed in Edwin's pocket, because Jasper *did not know it was there.*

A flash of lightning showed in the sky.

Joe reasoned that Charles Dickens might have meant for the ring to identify the body of Edwin Drood. The ring could not be dissolved by the quicklime, because it, too, was made of metal. In other words, sooner or later, the ring would speak the truth about what had happened to Edwin Drood.

That would be a fantastic conclusion to the story, Joe thought. *A ring that speaks the truth.*

Joe's thoughts melted into a feeling of sadness. Thinking about the engagement ring reminded him of his father's high-school ring, the one he had lost a few days ago.

I wish my father's ring could speak the truth about where it is. Who knows? Maybe it can. Maybe a metal detector would help it speak the truth. I know David has a metal detector. I'm sure . . .

Thoughts about a note floated into Joe's mind. It was the note he had seen in David's garage, the one that read: "Set for AU."

Wait! "AU" is the scientific symbol for gold. Maybe David wrote the note because he wanted to set his metal detector so it would pick up on the presence of gold—as a way of finding the ring.

Joe knew how badly David felt about the missing ring. In addition to that, the baseball cap was right along the path that he and David had taken when the ring was lost. The cap could easily have blown off David's head while he went back to search for the ring.

Joe looked down at Wishbone. "Maybe that's what David was doing today—searching for the ring with a metal detector!"

Wishbone looked up at Joe with alert eyes, almost as if he understood the words.

This theory did not explain where David was. It also didn't explain why David had not called Joe or Mrs. Barnes. But at least Joe felt he had a solid clue to follow.

Wishbone whipped his head around, as if he had heard someone coming. Through the thick wall of rain, Joe was able to see a figure running toward the train station. Only when the figure came under the roof of the waiting platform did Joe see that it was Sam. She was soaking wet, and her blond hair was plastered down.

"What are you doing here?" Joe said, standing up. "I thought you had to work at Pepper Pete's tonight."

"I do," Sam said, struggling to catch her breath. "But I've been worried sick about David. I guess you haven't found him, because you never called me. I saw you sitting outside the post office with Mr. Bloodgood a while ago. I wanted to come out of the pizza parlor and see what you were up to, but I had to finish serving a few customers first. By the time I was done, you were gone. I decided to go look for you. I just kept running until I found you here."

"Listen, I just came up with an idea," Joe said. "I think David might have been out searching for my dad's ring with a metal detector."

"Why do you think that?"

"I'll explain later. Right now—"

"Right now," Sam said, picking up on Joe's remark, "we just need to find him. Tell me where you think you might have lost the ring."

115

Joe held a hand to his forehead, thinking. "Okay, the day I lost the ring was the last day of school before the winter break. David and I got on our bikes at the school bike rack. We rode next to the railroad tracks for a while. Then we went inside the Hobrock Plant—you know, the abandoned factory. I *know* I had the ring on when I got onto my bike. And I . . . uh . . . discovered that it was missing when I was past the factory."

"So that means you lost the ring somewhere between the school and the factory. That means we might find David somewhere along that route."

"I didn't see any sign of him over by the school," Joe said. "So let's keep going until we get to the factory."

Joe, Sam, and Wishbone dashed into the pouring rain and began to run alongside the railroad tracks. The raindrops felt cold on Joe's face, and he could feel them quickly drenching his clothing. As Joe ran, he looked around in every direction, but there was not a single person in sight.

Soon Joe, Sam, and Wishbone arrived at the Hobrock Plant. It was a lonely brick building on the other side of the train tracks from where they were. The old factory had closed down years ago, but Joe and David had climbed inside through a window one day to have a look around the deserted building.

"Do you think David could be in there?" Sam said, raising her voice to be heard over the storm.

"Let's give it a try," Joe suggested.

Joe went to the window that he and David had climbed through on the day in question. The top pane was coated with grime, and the bottom pane was completely broken away. Joe lifted Wishbone carefully through the window with the missing pane. Then the dog jumped to the floor. Sam pulled herself up and climbed through the window. Next, Joe followed.

Joe stood in the factory, sopping wet, his clothing

dripping all over the floor. During the day, sunlight streamed through the grimy windows, but now the place was pitch-dark.

"Wow! It's really dark in here," Wishbone said.

Wishbone couldn't see a thing. But his nose was picking up all sorts of interesting scents—dust, rusted metal, old grease, a chemical smell, maybe a few spider webs.

"David, are you in here?" Joe called out. "David, it's me—Joe! Can you hear me?"

"David!" Sam called. "David Barnes, are you in here?"

The voices echoed in the deep, almost empty space. There was no reply except for the wild noise of the storm outside.

"Oh, that reminds me," Wishbone said. He gave his body a shake, throwing rainwater off his wet fur.

Something came clanging to the floor, barely missing Wishbone's paw.

"What was that?" Sam asked fearfully.

"I don't know," Joe whispered. "Probably a pipe or a can, or something like that. We need to be really careful."

"David didn't answer us," Sam told Joe. "Do you still think he could be in here?"

"It's possible," Joe said. "It's a big place. Let's explore a bit. But, remember, be very careful. There's no telling what we could run into."

As Joe and Sam moved around, Wishbone heard the wet squishing of their shoes on the concrete floor. Wishbone began to roam around, too. He was very careful about where he placed his paws. Soon the dog's eyes got used to the darkness. He sensed all sorts of ghostly shapes hanging around the space.

I wonder if any of those shapes are real ghosts, Wishbone thought with concern. *Who knows? This may even be where the spirit of Charles Dickens is staying while he's in town. I like to think about ghosts, but I don't enjoy being cooped up in a dark room with them. Then, again, those shapes probably just belong to old equipment that's never been taken out of the factory.*

Suddenly, Wishbone froze. He heard a very soft pattering noise.

Uh . . . maybe I spoke too soon.

As the noise came closer, Wishbone realized it was the patter of teeny-tiny feet. Every bit of fur on his back shot up as he went on full alert for trouble. The dog was just about to growl into the darkness. Then he suddenly recognized a faintly familiar odor.

You know what? I think I smell a—

"I think I heard a rat!" Sam cried out.

"Guess what," Joe said, sounding nervous. "I think I heard it, too."

"Hey, guys, don't worry," Wishbone assured his friends. "Rats are nothing to be worried— *Hellllppp!!!*"

The rat's bristly little body had brushed against Wishbone's front paw. With a high-pitched squeak, the rat went skittering away in the darkness.

"Yeah! You had better scram!" Wishbone called out after the rat. "I just happen to know a gray cat who would love—"

Wishbone stuck his nose up into the musty air. Among all the odors, he was suddenly picking up a new smell. It was completely different from the others because, except for Joe and Sam, it was the only human scent in the area. Wishbone took a few deep sniffs.

Hey! That's David's scent!

The aroma was quite fresh. That told Wishbone David had been in the factory sometime in the past few hours. Wishbone lowered his black nose to the ground, sniffing this way and that. Soon he picked up David's trail and began to follow it through the strange indoor darkness.

The dog knocked over a can, which gave a loud clatter as it smacked onto the concrete floor.

Wishbone followed David's scent down a few steps that led to another large work area. After walking across a long stretch of concrete floor, the dog found himself face to face with a door. Wishbone found a crack at the bottom of the door. He crouched down to give it a good sniff.

Eureka! I've found it!

"Joe!" Wishbone called out. "I think David is behind this door! In fact, I'm *sure* of it! I know that sometimes you may not be so sure about my instincts, but it's time to believe me now! Sam, you, too!"

Joe and Sam seemed to be too far away to hear.

Wishbone raised himself up onto his hind legs and pawed at the door. His nails scraped against the metal. "David, are you in there, buddy? Hey, David! If you're in there, open up!"

From the other side of the door, a voice called out, "Hello . . . is someone out there?"

Wishbone's heart seemed to leap upward. The dog *knew* it was David's voice. Wishbone began to bark.

Joe ran toward Wishbone's barking. He shouted, "David, is that you?"

"Joe?" David yelled back.

"Yes! It's me!" Joe called. "Sam is here, too!"

"I'm over here!" David called.

"We already know that," Wishbone said, wagging his tail excitedly.

Wishbone heard Joe and Sam's squishy footsteps moving quickly as they came closer to the door. Soon they were right beside it. Joe tried to turn the doorknob, but the door wouldn't budge.

"The door's stuck," David called. "There's no doorknob on my side, and I don't have anything to pry open the latch with. I've been trapped in here."

"What should we do?" Sam asked.

"Do either of you have your library card?" David asked.

"David, I know you're a good student," Wishbone commented, "but I hardly think this is the time—"

"Yes." Joe said.

"Stick it between the door and the frame," David told Joe, "about two inches above the doorknob. Then try to push the latch back."

Joe fished inside his pocket and pulled out his plastic library card. He spent a few minutes working carefully with the card at the side of the door. After muttering quite a few words of frustration, Joe finally was able to push back the latch. Then he opened the door. . . .

Joe, Sam, and Wishbone quickly stepped into the room. Even though it was very dark, Joe knew that the boy standing on the other side of the doorway was David Barnes.

"Are you okay?" Joe asked.

Through the thick darkness, Joe could sense that David was smiling. "Yeah. Considering the fact that I've been trapped alone in a cold, lonely, scary room for the past few hours, I guess I'm fine."

Joe felt a warm sense of relief flow through his body. He slapped David on the arm and said, "Good to see you, David!"

David slapped Joe back and said, "It's even better to see *you!*"

Without saying a word, Sam wrapped her arms around David, giving him a tight hug. Wishbone got on his hind legs to give David a few welcoming paw scratches.

When the greetings were over, David said, "How in the world did you guys ever find me?"

"Yes," Sam said, turning to Joe, "how in the world *did* you find him?"

"Believe it or not," Joe said, brushing back his wet hair, "I had a little help from *The Mystery of Edwin Drood.* I'll give you all the details later. But a little while ago, I finally figured out that David went looking for my lost ring—with a metal detector set to pick up the presence of gold."

"Of course!" Sam exclaimed. "'Set for AU'!"

Joe nodded. "When did you get the idea for that?" Joe asked David.

"Last night, when I was at your house," David said.

"Was that when I saw you staring out the window?" Joe said. "I asked what was on your mind, and you said it was nothing."

"That's right," David admitted. "Suddenly, I thought of a better way to look for the ring. I didn't tell you I was thinking about the ring, though, because I didn't want to get your hopes up. I figured if I actually found the ring, it would make a great surprise Christmas present."

"And the better way was to use a metal detector?" Sam asked.

David took a few steps. Then he picked something up, which he handed to Sam. Joe could see that it was a pole with some kind of device at one end.

"This is my metal detector," David explained. "I knew a metal detector just by itself wouldn't be enough to locate the ring. There are all kinds of metal between the school and this factory. The detector would have beeped every time I came near a penny or a bottle cap.

"But when I was at your house, I realized I might be able to adjust the metal detector so it would pick up only on gold. When I went home last night, I tinkered with my metal detector and I got it working just right. Then today, around noon, I began to search for the ring."

"I guess this was after you went to Mr. Pruitt's house?" Joe asked.

"How do you know about that?" David asked.

"We did some detective work," Joe said modestly. "But why did you go into this room? We didn't go into it the other day."

David spoke in an embarrassed tone of voice. "I got curious about the machines in here. They're powered by these really old diesel-style engines. Anyway, while I was checking them out, a gust of wind slammed the door shut. For at least two hours I tried with all my strength to get the door open. But I didn't have anything to use on the latch. Finally, I fell asleep. I'm so glad you thought of coming over to the door. Between my sleeping and the storm, you might have left the factory without me even hearing that you were around. I could have spent all night in here."

"I think you'd better give Wishbone some credit," Joe pointed out. "He's the one who went for the door."

David knelt down and gave Wishbone a scratch on the back. "I'll be happy to give the credit to Wishbone. I should probably also give him some treats."

Joe could hear Wishbone licking David's hand.

"There's one thing I don't understand," Sam told David. "Why didn't you phone and say you wouldn't be coming to our meeting today? Joe and I were worried about you."

"I *did* call," David said, sounding puzzled. "I left a message on the Talbots' answering machine. I said I wouldn't be coming to the *Edwin Drood* discussion group because I wanted to do some research on a project."

Joe rubbed his chin. "When did you call?"

"This morning," David answered. "A little after eleven. I waited until then because I didn't want the phone to disturb you in case you were sleeping late."

There was a pause.

Joe said, "David, are you *sure* you called?"

"Yes," David replied, "I'm positive."

"I came home a little before noon and checked the machine," Joe explained, "but there were no messages."

"Hmm . . ." Sam murmured. "That's mysterious."

"*Very* mysterious," Joe said quietly.

David gave Wishbone one final scratch. Then he stood up. "Even though it's raining cats and dogs, I'd better get home. I'm sure my mom's worried about me. And, I'm sorry to tell you, Joe, but I still haven't found the ring. However, I still have some ground to cover here in the factory. I'll come back tomorrow and keep looking."

Joe threw an arm around his friend's shoulder. "You know what? Even if you never find the ring, I really appreciate the fact that you've put so much effort into your search."

"Come on," Sam said joyfully, "let's get out of here."

The group made their way carefully through the darkness. As they walked, Joe told David about everything that had taken place earlier in the day. Joe could hear the wind howling outside. It was louder than ever.

Lightning flashed, briefly flooding the factory with light. In that split-second, Joe's eyes caught sight of something. He saw it in his mind even after darkness returned.

It was a glint of gold.

Could that be what I think it is? Joe thought, stopping in his tracks. *No—that would be way too strange.*

Joe peered through the cold darkness, trying to figure out exactly where the glint had been. As Joe concentrated, he heard Wishbone's nails clicking loudly on the concrete. After a few moments, Joe felt the dog nudging his head against his leg. Joe reached down to scratch Wishbone under his muzzle. As he did so, Wishbone dropped something into Joe's palm.

By the feel of it, Joe knew that it was his father's gold ring.

Chapter Fourteen

"That's a very nice-looking ring," Wishbone told Joe.

The storm was still raging, but Wishbone was dry and warm in the kitchen of the Talbot house. At the moment he was looking up at Joe, who was admiring his father's ring on his finger. Wishbone, Joe, and Ellen had just finished eating dinner. By then, Joe had filled Ellen in on all the details of the day. Wishbone had also added a few colorful comments.

Ellen began to clear the table. "I'm really very impressed to hear how much you cared about finding David. And I just love the fact that your library card saved the day."

"You'll have to mention it the next time you're at a librarians' conference," Joe said, getting up to help with the cleaning.

"I will," Ellen said with a laugh. "Anyway, I'm very proud of you. And I know that your dad would have been proud of you, too."

"I hope so," Joe said, looking at the ring again. He was now wearing it on his middle finger, instead of his ring finger. That way, there was no chance it could fall off.

Wishbone wagged his tail. The dog was very happy about the way the day had finally ended. Then his tail suddenly stopped in mid-wag. Wishbone quickly remembered something that he was *not* happy about. He had no idea at all where the pretzel-shaped rawhide bone was, or how to go about finding it.

I know Ellen is going to wrap up her presents tonight, Wishbone thought. *She's not going to be too pleased when she discovers that I borrowed that bone for a sneak preview.*

While Ellen continued to clean the kitchen, Wishbone watched her every move. All too soon, the dreaded moment came. Ellen wiped her hands on a dish towel and said to Joe, "I'm going to take care of some business in the study."

"Okay, Mom," Joe said, running a sponge over the kitchen table.

As Ellen walked out of the kitchen, Wishbone darted between her legs and ran for the study. Once there, he climbed onto the footstool, leaped onto the desk, walked across everything on it, then jumped down onto his big red chair.

When Ellen entered the study a moment later, Wishbone was sitting calmly in his chair. He was doing his best to imitate a gentleman sitting among his books.

"Why, hello, Ellen," Wishbone greeted her formally. "Welcome to the library. Do pull up a chair and make yourself comfortable."

"I probably shouldn't let you stay," Ellen told the dog, "but since you look so comfortable there . . ."

Ellen opened a drawer in the desk and pulled out wrapping paper, a pair of scissors, and tape. Then she opened the closet and pulled out some shopping bags. Wishbone figured the bags contained presents for Joe and some other people. The dog knew Ellen would be heading for the bookshelf next, where she had stashed the rawhide bone.

Delay her, no matter what, Wishbone thought.

"Say, Ellen," Wishbone said casually. "Suppose we read a book together. How about, say, the great Russian novel, *War and Peace?* It's only around a thousand pages long. We ought to be able to finish it by Christmas Eve. Or maybe New Year's Day."

Ellen didn't seem to hear. She did notice that a few books had fallen from the shelves onto the floor. Those were the books Wishbone had knocked down while searching for his present.

Do something!

Wishbone jumped down onto the floor and went into a crouching position, as if giving something a careful examination. "Uh-oh! I just spotted a flea on the floor. Ellen, you'd better leave the room at once and let me handle this."

Ellen looked curiously at the dog.

Wishbone crouched lower. "Yes, there are definitely fleas in here. This is terrible. But I'm sure I can handle the situation if you just leave the room at once!"

"Wishbone, why are you acting so strange?" Ellen asked.

Wishbone could see that Ellen wasn't buying the phony flea bit—at least, not yet. He sat down and scratched his side wildly, the way he did whenever he had experienced a flea invasion.

"Oh, no! They got me! But it's not too late for you to save yourself. Run for your life, Ellen—before it's too late!"

Ellen knelt down to Wishbone and checked his fur. "Do you have fleas? Hold still for a second and let me get a good look. . . . No . . . I don't see anything. If you keep scratching this way, though, I'd better consider giving you a flea bath."

One of Wishbone's least favorite things was the dreaded flea bath. He stopped scratching immediately and said, "Hey, you know what, Ellen? I was only joking about the fleas. Heh-heh! See? I'm fine! One hundred percent flea-free!"

Ellen looked at the fallen books again. She saw that some of them had come from a lower shelf. Then she noticed that others had come from a higher shelf—the shelf where The Bone had been hidden. Wishbone noticed a look of suspicion forming on Ellen's face.

Do something else. Anything! Fast!

Wishbone nudged Ellen's leg. "Say, Ellen, would you care to dance? Let me show you how to do the latest dance, called the four-step."

Ellen turned to Wishbone and narrowed her eyes. "Were you snooping around in here today?"

Wishbone pretended he hadn't heard her question. "You know, you and I haven't danced together in the longest time. Come to think of it, you and I have *never* danced together. And that's a real shame. Because dancing is a lot of fun. Good exercise, too. So, what'll it be? Tango? Disco? Rumba? Dog trot?"

Ellen spotted the space where Wishbone had found his present. She reached inside the space and felt around with her hand.

She looked at Wishbone with a serious expression. "Wishbone, do you know where a certain pretzel-shaped rawhide bone might be?"

By that time, Wishbone was in the middle of the room doing some footwork that resembled dancing. "Are you talking to me? Oh, sorry, I'm just practicing a few new steps. They don't call me the John Travolta of terriers for nothing."

"Where is that bone?" Ellen asked again.

"Bone?" Wishbone said, as he continued to dance. "What bone?"

Ellen sighed. "I was afraid you would find it. That's why I didn't hide it with the other presents in the closet. But it seems pretty clear that you got to it, anyway. Can you at least show me where it is?"

Wishbone stopped dancing. He could see that his game was over. There was nothing left to do except tell the truth.

"Yes, I took the bone," he admitted simply. "But I have no idea on earth—or under it, for that matter—where it is now. For all I know, it disappeared into thin air. I guess this is another one of those mysteries like *The Mystery of Edwin Drood*. A mystery that will never be fully solved. There's something in the wind, I tell you."

As Ellen's serious look melted away, she bent down and scratched Wishbone behind the ears. "Well, I guess I'll have to buy you something else. I'm not happy about what you've done. . . . Still, in this house everyone gets a present under the tree."

Chapter Fifteen

A gigantic evergreen Christmas tree towered high above the courtyard outside Oakdale's public library. Wishbone couldn't stop admiring all the brightly colored lights and beautiful ornaments on the tree. The strings of popcorn Ellen had made for the tree looked good enough to eat. In fact, Wishbone was considering sampling a few pieces.

The night was clear, cold, but very calm. Wishbone was relieved that the mysterious wind had completely vanished. He figured it was probably off causing trouble in some other town by then.

Many of Oakdale's residents had gathered for the tree-lighting ceremony. The tree had been officially lit a few minutes ago. Now a single elf was passing out treat packages to the smaller kids. The elf was Wanda, dressed in a green costume with different-colored bells jangling on her sleeves and shoes.

Wishbone was standing in the middle of a small group made up of Joe, Sam, and David. As Wanda passed by, Sam said, "Miss Gilmore, you're the best elf this side of the North Pole."

"Why, thank you, Samantha," Wanda said, jingling some bells on her sleeve. "The only ones I could find who

131

were interested in being elves were little kids. But that was no good, because the little kids are the ones the elves are supposed to be handing treats to. So I figured I could just do the whole elf thing myself. And I'm having a great time with it. I might even add this costume to my regular everyday wardrobe."

As everyone had a good laugh, Wanda returned to her merry elf duties.

Luis and Lola approached the group. "Hi, everybody," Luis greeted them. "Lola and I had a lot of fun with you guys last night at Pepper Pete's."

"Same here," David said, shaking hands with Luis. In fact, it was so much fun that maybe we should do it again tonight."

"Sounds good to me," Lola said, putting an arm around Sam. "Of all the places I've eaten at in this country, Pepper Pete's is one of the best."

Wishbone wagged his tail. "I'll agree with that. And just wait until you try the spicy Italian sausage topping!"

"And remember," Luis told Joe. "Tomorrow it's you and me for a one-on-one basketball match."

"I'll be there," Joe said with a nod.

Chloe came over and immediately went to David. "Hi, David," she said, fixing her blue eyes on him. "Did I hear you just say all of you were going to Pepper Pete's tonight?"

David scratched his neck, seeming a little embarrassed. "Uh . . . yeah, that's right. Do you . . . uh . . . want to come along?"

Chloe's face lit up like a lightbulb. "Oh, I'd love to!"

Wishbone nudged Joe's leg and whispered, "So, does David like this girl or not? I still don't think she's his type, but, you know, he keeps inviting her places."

"Hey, Joe," Chloe called over. "Do you know who you remind me of these days?"

"Uh . . . who?" Joe asked.

"Santa Claus!" Chloe said, releasing her bird-chirp laugh.

Joe blushed, and Sam smiled.

"Well, it's time for me to get to work," David said, pulling himself away from Chloe.

Wishbone watched David go to a collection of electrical equipment he had set up at the other end of the courtyard. Soon a voice behind the tree was heard bellowing. "Yo-ho-ho! Merry Christmas! Yo-ho-ho-ho!"

Light appeared on a small platform stage that stood directly in front of the tree. As the crowd cheered, Santa Claus jumped up onto the stage. To Wishbone, it looked exactly like the real Santa Claus, even though the dog knew very well that it was actually Mr. Pruitt. After a few words of greeting, Santa sat in a chair, opened a book, and began to read from the famous Christmas poem "A Visit from Saint Nicholas."

In a dramatic manner, Mr. Pruitt spoke:

> *'Twas the night before Christmas,*
> *When all through the house,*
> *Not a creature was stirring, not even a mouse....*

Joe knew Mr. Pruitt did a terrific job with the poem. But he had heard it for the past five years. Right now there was something else on his mind. Joe led Sam and Wishbone to David's sound-and-light station at the rear of the crowd.

"We still haven't gotten around to having our official *Edwin Drood* discussion," Joe told his friends. "But I've got my theories all ready to go, and I'm eager to tell you what they are."

"I've got my theories all ready, too," Sam said.

"Make that three," David added.

"Cool," Joe said. "Okay, I'll go first. I think John Jasper really *did* murder Edwin Drood. He wanted Rosa Bud all to himself. I guess you might say it's kind of like the way Chloe wants David."

"Oh, give me a break," David said, rolling his eyes.

"Well, I think Jasper *meant* to kill Edwin," Sam said. "But instead of really doing it, he only *imagined* he did it, while he was in a deep opium trance. I got the idea from Mr. Pruitt. When I watched him rehearsing his Elvis act, I saw how deeply some people can enter into their double life."

David displayed a proud look. "I think Jasper *tried* to kill Edwin. But Edwin fought to get free. Then he went into hiding for a while. I got my idea when I was stuck in the factory. When I was trying to get that door open, I realized how hard a person will fight for his own survival."

"We're all very glad you're alive," Joe said. He gave his friend a playful slap on the arm. Joe said this in a joking way, but he reminded himself always to appreciate his friends.

"Now," Sam said, pretending to stroke a long beard, "let's discuss the identity of the detective, Dick Datchery."

Joe jumped in. "I think Dick Datchery was Neville Landless. He was trying to clear his name because everyone in Cloisterham thought he had murdered Edwin. I think I got that idea from talking to Luis. He made me see how badly newcomers want to be accepted in a new town."

"That's funny," Sam said, "because I think Dick Datchery was Helena Landless. She was trying to clear her brother's name because she cared about him so much. I got that idea when Joe told me how worried Lola was about Luis."

"I think Dick Datchery was Edwin Drood," David said. "You see, he was trying to gather evidence against Jasper to make sure Jasper got thrown into prison for the murder attempt. Having been a missing person myself lately, I think I've gained some understanding of ol' Edwin."

"What do you know?" Joe said with a pleased smile. "We've all got great theories, and they're all different from each other."

"Too bad we'll never know the real truth," David said. "Unless we get visited by the spirit of Charles Dickens."

Wishbone raised up onto his hind legs and pawed at Joe's pants.

"Look," Joe said with a laugh, "I think Wishbone is giving us his own theory."

"What a shame he doesn't speak English," Sam remarked.

"Hey! Didn't you guys hear what I said?" Wishbone exclaimed. "For barking out loud, I just gave you the correct outcome to *The Mystery of Edwin Drood*! And I think we *were* visited by the spirit of Charles Dickens! Tell me, why is it that no one *ever* listens to the dog?!"

After a glance at Mr. Pruitt, David knelt down beside the electrical equipment. "I think you will want to watch what's coming up next."

Wishbone, Joe, and Sam turned to watch the stage. Soon Mr. Pruitt was delivering the poem's final lines:

> . . . but I heard him exclaim, 'ere he drove out of sight,
> Happy Christmas to all, and to all a good night.

Applause broke out among the audience. Suddenly, green and red lights were spotlighted on Mr. Pruitt. The lights then flickered around the stage in continuous motion. As rock-and-roll music burst forth from loudspeakers, Mr. Pruitt kicked off his boots, unfastened his big black belt, and removed his Santa costume.

There were quite a few gasps in the crowd when

people saw that Mr. Pruitt was wearing the glimmering silver jumpsuit. Next, Mr. Pruitt pulled off his cap, white hair, and white beard to reveal his black Elvis wig. Finally, he reached down and picked up a microphone.

The shock of the audience was great. Mr. Pruitt began to sing and wiggle his hips. He was no longer a mild-mannered schoolteacher, but now—he had changed into Elvis Presley!

Deck the halls with boughs of holly,
Fa-la-la-la-la-la-la-la-la.

Chloe and her group of friends from the church party rushed toward the stage, screaming and cheering with delight. The sounds were so loud and high-pitched that Wishbone was forced to fold down his ears.

Wishbone caught a glimpse of Wanda, who held both hands to her cheeks with astonishment. "Oh, my goodness!" she cried out. "This is fantastic! He's brought

back Elvis! We've never had anything like *this* at our tree-lighting ceremony!"

As Mr. Pruitt continued to sing and wiggle, the entire crowd went wild with excitement. Even Wishbone had to admit that Mr. Pruitt had changed himself into a very convincing Elvis impersonator. By the time Mr. Pruitt came to the carol's third and final verse, most everyone was singing along. Wishbone tilted his muzzle upward and howled along, too.

> *Fast away the old year passes,*
> *Fa-la-la-la-la-la-la-la-la.*
> *Hail the new, ye lads and lasses.*
> *Fa-la-la-la-la-la-la-la-la.*

Joe knelt down and put a friendly hand on Wishbone's back. The dog raised his voice even louder.

> *Sing we joyous all together,*
> *Fa-la-la-la-la-la-la-la-la.*
> *Heedless of the wind and weather,*
> *Fa-la-la-la-la-la-la-la-laaaaa!*

When the song ended, everyone clapped and cheered. There was even some hugging going on.

Well, everything turned out great, Wishbone thought, as he watched the merrymaking. *But, you know, this has been the most mysterious holiday season I can remember. That wind definitely blew some strangeness into town. I guess all the mysteries have been solved, though—except for the missing bone. Where in the world did that thing go? And, oh, yes, there's another unsolved mystery. What happened to that message David left on the phone machine?*

Mr. Pruitt spoke into the mike, still using his Elvis voice. "I wanna thank y'all for comin' out tonight.

137

Everyone, I hope ya have a rockin' Christmas and a rollin' New Year!"

Once again, Chloe and her friends screamed with delight. A little girl nearby jumped up and down, almost stepping on one of Wishbone's paws.

"Hey, watch it!" Wishbone warned the girl. "You might step on someone or something that wasn't meant to be stepped on!"

An idea rang like a bell in Wishbone's mind.

Wait!

Wishbone thought back to the time when he was searching through the study for his present. He remembered jumping onto the desk and walking across a bunch of things. One of those items he had stepped on was the telephone answering machine.

Whoops! I'll bet that's what happened to David's message. I know if you just touch those machines in the wrong place, all the messages can be erased. I must have accidentally stepped on the Erase button. . . .

Members of the crowd began to say their good-byes and clear out of the courtyard. Wanda, Ellen, Joe, Sam, and David went to congratulate Mr. Pruitt on his spectacular performance.

Wishbone gave his side a thoughtful scratch. *In a way, I guess all that fuss over David was all my fault. But then, if Joe had gotten that message, we never would have gone looking for David. And David might have been trapped in that factory a lot longer.*

If you look at it that way, I was a hero!

Wishbone saw Joe signal for him to join the group.

Should I tell the others about this, or just keep quiet about the matter? Hmm, I think I'll just keep quiet. You never know how humans are going to react. We can let this be another one of those mysteries that remains a mystery . . . forever.

About Alexander Steele

Alexander Steele is a writer of books, plays, and screenplays, for both children and adults . . . and sometimes for dogs. *Case of the Unsolved Case* is his third book for the WISHBONE Mysteries series. His first two titles were *Tale of the Missing Mascot* and *Case of the On-Line Alien*. He has also written *Moby Dog* for The Adventures of Wishbone series.

Mystery and history are favorite subjects for Alexander. He has written ten detective novels for children. He is currently working on a novel for adults that deals with the origin of detectives in both fiction and real life. Among Alexander's plays is the award-winning *One Glorious Afternoon*, which features Shakespeare and his fellow players at London's Globe Theatre.

Alexander first became familiar with Charles Dickens when, as a young boy, he appeared in a stage version of *Oliver!*, based on Dickens's great tale *Oliver Twist*. Soon Dickens became one of Alexander's favorite authors. He especially likes the way Dickens weaves together elements of comedy and drama.

Alexander didn't read *The Mystery of Edwin Drood* until he began to write *Case of the Unsolved Case*. He wonders if any of the solutions suggested by Joe, Sam, and David are what Mr. Dickens had in mind for his final and most mysterious book.

Alexander lives in New York City, which has more unsolved mysteries than Cloisterham.

Coming Soon!

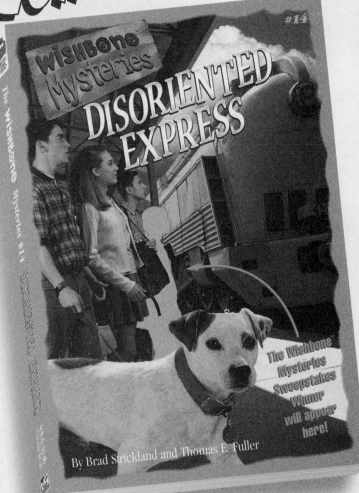

#14

WISHBONE Mysteries

DISORIENTED EXPRESS

The Wishbone Mysteries Sweepstakes Winner will appear here!

By Brad Strickland and Thomas E. Fuller

The Adventures of WISHBONE

Read all the books in
The Adventures of Wishbone™ series!